Duet

Duet

ELISE BROACH

with illustrations by Ziyue Chen

Christy Ottaviano Books

LITTLE, BROWN AND COMPANY
New York Boston

Christy Ottaviano Books
Hachette Book Group
1290 Avenue of the Americas, New York, NY 10104
Visit us at LBYR.com

First Edition: May 2022

Christy Ottaviano Books is an imprint of Little, Brown and Company. The Christy Ottaviano
Books name and logo are trademarks of Hachette Book Group, Inc.

The publisher is not responsible for websites (or their content) that are not owned by the publisher.

Library of Congress Cataloging-in-Publication Data
Names: Broach, Elise, author.
Title: Duet / Elise Broach.
Description: First edition. | New York : Little, Brown and Company, 2022. | Audience: Ages 8–12.
| Summary: The life of a musically gifted bird changes forever after she discovers the music of
Chopin and helps a talented young pianist solve the mystery of a long-lost Chopin piano.
Identifiers: LCCN 2021010563 | ISBN 9780316311359 (hardcover) | ISBN 9780316311557 (ebook)
Subjects: CYAC: Goldfinches—Fiction. | Birdsongs—Fiction. | Music—Fiction. | Chopin,
Frédéric, 1810–1849—Fiction. | Piano—Fiction. | Human-animal relationships—Fiction.
Classification: LCC PZ7.B78083 Du 2022 | DDC [Fic]—dc23
LC record available at https://lccn.loc.gov/2021010563

ISBNs: 978-0-316-31135-9 (hardcover), 978-0-316-31155-7 (ebook)

Printed in the United States of America

LSC-C

Printing 1, 2022

In memory of my dear friend, the poet
Ann Victoria Christie, lover of birds and words

Contents

1

Music Lesson

Call me Mirabelle. It's a nice name, don't you think? We all have pretty names, my mother says, because we're all beautiful. Every last one of us! There's no such thing as an ugly goldfinch. We're little and yellow, with gray, black, and white markings. But it's mostly the yellow you notice: like a beam of sunshine, or a marigold, or a lemon. Just seeing me—even for a split second, half hidden by leaves, a glimpse of that bright, flashing yellow—well, I promise you, it is guaranteed to make you smile.

Okay, I admit, my brothers are an even brighter color than I am. The boys always are. Why *is* that? So annoying. They brag about it, too. But Mother says we girls have *subtlety* in our yellow hues. I like the sound of that. A subtle yellow is more elegant, I'm pretty sure.

And I'm still yellow enough to brighten the grayest day. Early in the spring, when the old man, Mr. Starek, was sick, I sat on a branch outside his bedroom window to cheer him up. It had been a sad winter for him. His sister died, and even though she lived close by, they hadn't seen each other in years and years. Isn't that strange? I can't imagine not seeing my brothers for years, although they do make me mad sometimes.

We all knew Mr. Starek was very upset. In a way, that surprised me. If he hadn't seen his sister in such a long time, why would he miss her now that she was gone? But he *did* miss her. He has no other family, from what we can tell…maybe relatives far away, in Europe, but not here in America. There's a photograph of his sister in his bedroom, and after she died, he would look at it sorrowfully for long periods. And then there was some trouble with her house. I'm not sure what exactly—something involving money, and birds have no interest in money, so we didn't pay much attention. But the old man got sick in the middle of all this, and Mother told me to visit him. It seemed like the least I could do, since he always fills the bird feeder for us.

Sometimes I would sing for him. The high limb of a dogwood tree grazes his window, so I would hop to the end of it, close to the pane, and then let the song pour out of me—like water rippling or wind blowing through tall grass, something so free and fast and flowing that it can't be stopped. The old man would startle in his bed and turn toward the window, and then he'd listen intently. I

2

could see the concentration in his face. I don't think I'm flattering myself when I say he looked impressed, like hearing me sing was a real tweet. Haha, *treat*, I mean. Bird joke. For a singer, there is no greater compliment than someone who truly listens to you.

I'm a musical artist, you see. I prefer *artiste*, actually. It sounds more distinguished. All of us goldfinches can sing, of course, but I'm not like the rest of them, with their wild racket of chirping. I still have a lot of practicing to do, but I promise you this: when I sing, anyone within earshot knows it's a *song*.

Which is why I like the old man. Mr. Starek appreciates music. He's a music teacher, a pianist. And from what I can tell, he used to be *famous*. He played the piano all over the world! Can you imagine? Packed on the shelves of his music room are shiny trophies and serious-looking plaques with his name on them. And hanging on the walls are framed pictures of the world's great composers. How do I know they're the world's great composers? Well, he plays their music on his piano, and I have ears, don't I?

And something more important, which you can't really teach: taste. Musical taste. I grew up listening to the old man play— Beethoven and Mozart and Brahms and Bach—and hearing him talk about music, week after week, to the piano students who came through his front door. Now, since he got sick, he's pretty much stopped teaching. Parents come begging for lessons and he tells them he's retired. But I learned a lot while he was still giving piano lessons. He'd say things like:

3

"This is Beethoven's Moonlight Sonata. Movement one starts gently, softly, like a lullaby."

Or:

"You need speed and delicacy for Debussy. When you touch the keys, imagine they are covered in flecks of gold. Pick up the flecks as quickly as possible."

See what I mean? For him, even talking about music is an art. It doesn't hurt that he has an accent. Mother says he's from Europe, a place called Poland, and he has a careful way of speaking that makes everything he says sound smart.

"I wish I had an accent," I tell Mother.

"You do have an accent," she says. "You just can't hear it. If you flew all the way to Europe, you'd sound different to the birds over there."

Isn't that funny? We all have accents! We just don't know it until we go someplace where people don't talk the same way we do.

The children used to come to the old man's house almost every afternoon. Most of them lived in Boston, which is a big, red-and-gray city about an hour from here, flying time. Remember, we birds don't have to follow roads or stop for traffic lights, so we can get to places a lot faster than you humans can.

Anyway, the children's parents would bring them all the way out to Mr. Starek's little town for their lessons. A sweet-smelling silk tree grows near the music room, and I would perch on the bottom limb and watch the lessons through the window. I could see everything from there. I would sit perfectly still and listen, because listening is the best kind of learning for me. And birds have excellent hearing—did you know that? Of the five senses, it's our second-best, after sight. I can hear the piano perfectly even with the windows closed, and when I'm swept up in it, the music fills me almost the way it does when I'm singing. It swirls around me, sliding through my feathers like water, wave after wave washing into my *soul*.

Oh, you didn't think birds had souls? Of course we do.

With the music lessons, the children did get better over time, but they were never as good as the old man. I think we artists are the only ones who really know what it takes. And we recognize it in each other. Even now, when Mr. Starek goes into the music room and sits at the piano, his fingers dance over the keys, quickly, softly, and then with force: *ba-ta-ta-DUM!* I see his body sway and his arms tense and then loosen as his long fingers span the keys. I feel the music beat in me like a second heart. Oh my goodness, does it make me want to *sing*.

Sometimes the old man glances up and sees me. I think he can tell how excited I am. I miss the piano lessons he used to give. Honestly, I learned so much from them. The old man would often play a short piece for the child at the beginning of the lesson, and I loved listening to him.

Sometimes, even now, after he plays for a bit, he'll walk to the window to speak to me.

"Hello, little bird. Are you hungry?" he'll say. "I filled the bird feeder for you."

I pretend to be shy. If he comes too close, I hop backward on the branch and then fly away home to the shiny green holly tree.

It grows by the fence in his backyard, and it's where I live with my mother and brothers.

I'm not shy, really. None of us birds are, but people like it when we pretend to be. Don't get me wrong…birds are careful of dangerous situations. We look out for ourselves. But that whole elaborate dance—hopping close to a person, then flying away, then returning and approaching even closer, then fluttering off again? I'll let you in on a secret. It's a performance. People like to feel chosen, like they've been singled out for a wild creature's attention and trust.

You don't believe me? One word for you: pigeons. Pigeons aren't shy at all. They flock to people, and how do people react? Everybody thinks pigeons are very ordinary. Worse yet, people are annoyed by them and call them pests. So believe me, the rest of us birds learned our lesson. Pretend to be shy.

That's what I do with the old man. When he comes to the window and talks to me, I quickly hop up the branch, cock my head at him, and then, with a whoosh, I flutter away.

Here's another thing I bet you're dying to know: what it's like to fly. Well, I won't lie to you. Flying is THE BEST. Next to singing, it is the most wonderful feeling you can imagine. Mother says we must never take it for granted, and I promise not to.

How can I describe it?

When I lift off from a branch, my wings are beat-beat-beating, super fast.

Currents of air rush underneath me, and it's like being lifted by a cloud—something weightless but also thick, cushioning my body and streaming off my wings and pulling me, pushing me, raising me higher and higher and higher.

And then, when I'm high enough, I dive and float and soar, buoyed only by air.

The whole world spreads out beneath me. I can see the entire backyard of the Garcias, the family who lives next door to Mr. Starek: their swing set, their deck, their barbecue grill. I can see the clumpy tops of trees, the bright flowerpots, the lush green squares of lawn, sometimes a turquoise swimming pool. I can see the colorful metal flashes of cars driving by, the geometry of streets and driveways in the neighborhood. And often, more often than I'd like, I can see the old man's fluffy gray cat, Harmony, sitting on the back patio, watching me.

I'm not scared of that old cat. What's there to be scared of, when you can *fly*?

In fact, on this sunny summer day, I am just about to execute a couple of loop-the-loops over Harmony's head, to remind her that she will never catch me. But then I see a boy.

His mother gets out of a car in the driveway, and she has to do some coaxing even to get the boy to join her.

Is he a piano student? I've never seen him before. He looks to be about eleven or twelve, though I admit, I am not good at guessing human ages. His hair is smooth and shining black, the blue-black of a raven's wing.

I land in the top twigs of the old yew bush by the front door for a better view. The boy is frowning, his face angry and clenched.

"I don't see why I can't keep taking lessons from Emily," he says.

"Michael," his mother says, her voice low, her arm urging him toward the old man's porch. "We've been through this. Emily is the one who thinks you need a new teacher. And years ago, Mr. Starek was *her* teacher. Think of that! You'll be taking lessons from your teacher's teacher."

Well, I hate to disappoint these two, but the old man is retired. They've come to the wrong place.

"I want Emily," the boy says. His hands ball into fists at his sides. He stops walking.

His mother sighs and bends down, her voice tight with exasperation. "I know you like Emily. She was an excellent teacher for you, all through elementary school. But she believes you have a real gift! She doesn't want to hold you back."

"She wasn't holding me back," the boy, Michael, says, still frowning.

I hop to a lower branch. This would be something new: a boy with real musical talent who doesn't want to take lessons from the old man. The old man is a very popular piano teacher. Before he got sick and stopped teaching, there was a long list of students waiting to study with him. I know this because, even now, they sometimes come to the house with their parents, or if they're teenagers, on their own, pleading with him to teach them piano. And he says no. Politely, of course—the old man is always polite. So why should this boy—this reluctant, grouchy boy—get the chance to study with him?

Is it because of his "gift"? If his mother and this Emily they're talking about are even right about that. Personally, I doubt it. The boy clearly doesn't want to be here, and the ones who have real talent can't wait to play.

Take me, for example. You couldn't keep me from singing if you tied my beak shut with string! That's the difference between an ordinary skill and a gift. A gift is an *obsession*. You can't stop yourself.

So why is the boy being so stubborn? His mother looks mad now, too. She reminds me of my mother when my brothers and I are splashing too long in the stone birdbath.

"Michael, please. Emily says Mr. Starek is the best of the best. And we're very lucky he's close by! At least let's go in and meet him."

"I like Emily," Michael says, his voice loud.

"Well, Emily likes Mr. Starek. And she thinks he'll be the perfect teacher for you. Let's give him a chance, okay?"

The mother presses the boy forward, herding him up the steps. She knocks on the door, then hesitantly clangs the large brass bell that hangs next to it.

"No one is better than Emily," Michael grumbles.

"Shhhh," the mother whispers, just as the old man opens the door.

He stands there smiling, in his pressed shirt and trousers, filling the doorframe. The old man is so distinguished looking. It is another thing I like about him: even on the quiet days, when he has no visitors, he dresses neatly, buffs his shoes, combs his hair.

"Ah, you must be Michael. Come in, come in." The old man swings the door wide. "Emily Goldberg told me all about you."

"Mr. Starek? We're so happy to meet you," the boy's mother says. Her voice sounds nervous. "I'm Vivian Jin, Michael's mother. I so appreciate you making an exception for Michael. I know you're not really teaching anymore."

Mr. Starek smiles faintly. "Well, Emily is very persuasive. And for the right student—"

"I have a teacher," the boy says to him, his face a stubborn scowl. "My teacher is Emily."

This boy is so rude! I want Mr. Starek to slam the door in his face.

But the old man does the opposite, welcoming him into the house. "Yes, I know," he says. "She was very enthusiastic about your playing. She says you have a real talent for Chopin."

It's a French name, Chopin. It's pronounced *show-pan*. I know this because Mr. Starek is something of a Chopin expert.

The old man tilts his head, studying the boy. "I understand you have only ten weeks to prepare for the Chopin Festival in Hartford."

Ooooh, a festival! I do love a festival.

"That's right," Mrs. Jin says. "And Emily says Chopin is your specialty. The festival is in mid-September. Do you think it's enough time?"

"We will see," Mr. Starek says. "We will see."

Mrs. Jin hesitates in the doorway. "Shall I stay…or…?"

"No, no, that's not necessary," the old man tells her. "Michael will be fine. Let's keep it to half an hour today, just an introduction. Michael, why don't you go into the music room? It's that door on the left."

The boy glances back at his mother, his face stormy, and skulks into the house.

Mrs. Jin shakes her head, her mouth a grim line. Now she seems more worried than mad. "I'm so sorry," she says. "He's not usually like this. He really does love to play."

Mr. Starek nods. "Emily tells me she's never had a student like him."

Michael's mother sighs. "It's been a hard year for him. His father took a job with an enormous amount of travel, and he won't be home this summer. I think Michael misses him, and he's nervous about starting middle school in the fall. It's…a lot of changes."

Mr. Starek studies her sympathetically. "I will be gentle with him."

"Thank you. I appreciate it."

Mrs. Jin turns to leave, and the door closes with a soft click.

I can tell the old man is going to have his work cut out for him with this one. But I can't help feeling curious. I want to hear the boy play.

2

Michael

Michael. It sounds a bit like Mirabelle, don't you think? It's musical in the same way, starting with a hum, ending with a trill. As I fly to my perch on the silk tree, I am wondering if this boy can live up to his musical name.

There are basically three kinds of piano students, I've found. There are the ones who don't want to be here, who come only because their parents make them. They may be good at the piano—sometimes really good—because the old man doesn't teach anyone who isn't, but they have no passion. They can learn how to play well technically, but they don't really care about the music, and they have no drive to be great.

Then there are the ones who want to be here and who try

really hard, listening to the old man and watching his fingers move on the keys and doing exactly what he tells them to. They care, and they want so badly to play well. They put in the time, and they get better and better. But they still lack something... that magical spark of talent. Even when they play a piece perfectly, what you hear is the effort, how carefully and purposefully they're playing it.

The last kind of students are the ones who play naturally. They may not work as hard, and sometimes I can tell they don't practice as much as they should, but when they're at the piano, you can feel the difference: a shimmer of something thrilling in the air. What you hear is the *music*, not the playing. And the music seems to have a life and mind and soul of its own.

That's what the old man must have been like as a boy.

And I wonder, because of what the mother said, is that what *this* boy is like? Right now, as I peer through the window, I see his glowering face and tense shoulders, the way he sits stiffly on the piano bench. He looks much more like the first kind of student, the one who's only here because somebody forced him to be.

But I won't know for sure till I hear him play. So I wait on the lowest branch of the silk tree, with the soft pink blossoms frothing around me.

The old man speaks softly to him. "Emily told me you've made great strides with Chopin over the last year, Michael. She says you're almost ready to compete—is that right?"

The boy doesn't say anything. He nods, almost imperceptibly.

"Would you like to play something?"

The boy shakes his head firmly.

"Well," the old man says, "why don't you take a few minutes and get to know the piano? This is an Érard. They're wonderful instruments—Chopin often played on one himself."

I see a flicker of curiosity cross the boy's face. But he sits unmoving, staring at the keys.

The old man waits, one hand resting on the polished wood top of the piano. "Try it. It's difficult to hit a wrong note."

Michael says nothing. His hands stay stiffly at his sides.

This is hardly a promising beginning, I think.

Finally, the old man says, "I'll leave you to it, shall I? Take your time." He walks into the hallway and closes the door behind him.

Michael sits at the piano, frozen. Why, if he were in a park, I would think he was a statue and I might land on his head. He doesn't so much as touch the keys.

What new sort of madness is this? The boy is here for lessons, very expensive lessons (as I happen to know from hearing the parents of Mr. Starek's previous students mutter about the cost). There's a competition coming up! And he isn't even going to play?

Come on, I want to shout. *What's the holdup? Let's see what you've got, kid.*

But do you know what? That boy does not play a single note.

Now, don't get me wrong. It's not as if he stays sitting on the bench. Once the old man is out of earshot, in some distant part of the house, the boy looks at the walls of the music room. After a minute, he stands up and starts poking around.

He's got a lot of nerve, right? He spends a long time with the piano, peering at it closely, inspecting the keyboard and the pedals underneath, tapping the wood. *Just play it*, I want to tell him. But then he drifts over to the books on the shelves, takes one out, thumbs through it. He picks up a plaque, then picks up a trophy. It's heavier than he expects and he almost drops it. That would be a fine mess, if he broke one of the old man's trophies. Then I bet the lessons would be off.

He walks around the piano, squeezing behind it, and I can't see what he's doing, so I hop a little closer to the windowpane to spy on him. Now, I have to tell you, I'm very small, petite really, but I weigh a lot more than the tree blossoms do. So when I hop, my weight on the branch makes the twiggy end of it scratch the window. Oops!

The boy whips around at the noise. He stares in my direction.

At first, I think he hasn't seen me. But then his whole face brightens.

What did I tell you about goldfinches? Guaranteed to make you smile.

He comes out from behind the piano and walks straight toward me. I think about flying away—my shy routine—but something stops me.

I want to see. I want to be seen.

So I stay right where I am and tilt my head to one side, giving him my prettiest look: bright-eyed, curious. I am summoning all of my charm.

And he just looks back at me, with his dark eyes and shining black wing of hair.

And then what do you think he does?

Bang!

His knuckles hit the glass.

"Go away, bird."

3

Back at the Nest

I have never been so insulted in my life! Honestly. Who does he think he is?

Of course, I immediately fly away. It's an instinctive reaction—because it was such a loud noise! So startling and unpleasant. I promise myself that's the LAST TIME that boy will get such a good look at me.

Let me tell you something: there are plenty of kids who like nothing better than to throw rocks at birds or try to catch us. Can you imagine? It's so mean. But this one…he should be different. He plays the *piano*. He's a musical artist, like me! Or he's supposed to be.

Oh, I am extremely disappointed. It makes me think he will not be much of a piano player after all.

I fly right back to the holly tree where Mother is building a nest.

You might think a holly is too prickly a home for us goldfinches, but actually, that's what makes it such a good choice. The sharp leaves don't bother us, and they keep other animals away. Plus, in winter, the bush will have yummy red berries for us to eat. (Don't try that yourself! Holly berries are poisonous to humans, especially if you eat a lot of them. But we goldfinches find them delicious.)

"Mirabelle! Where have you been all day?" Mother says when I flutter down to the nest.

"There's a new boy at the old man's house. He's going to take lessons," I tell her.

"Is he any good?" Mother asks, not so much because she cares but because she knows I do.

"I can't tell," I say. "He refused to play anything."

She's distracted, working on the nest, tidying up strands of grass and vines, smoothing them with her beak. Mother is about to lay a clutch of eggs, so the nest has to be ready for new babies. My brothers and I were born last year, in this very holly tree. Not far from where Mother is building the new nest, I can still see the broken remnants of the old one.

There was a terrible thunderstorm two nights ago, and in the lashing rain and wind, one side of the new nest broke apart. That doesn't happen often. Goldfinch nests are so sturdy and strong they can actually hold water! Like one of your human cups—just think about that—even though they're only made of plants and thistledown and sticky spiderwebs.

Here's another thing humans often seem confused about: you think of a nest as a bird's home. Actually, it's just a place to lay eggs and hatch chicks. Once the chicks can fly, the nest is abandoned, which is why you sometimes find old nests, long empty, in trees or under the eaves of porches. A bird's home—where we sleep at night—is called a *roost*. And it's usually just a tree or a bush, where we sleep standing up, holding on to a branch with our feet.

How many humans can do that? None, I bet. Goldfinches are very social, so we roost with our aunts and uncles and cousins and friends. And fathers too, usually, but our father happens to have what Mother calls a case of wanderlust, which means he takes off for long stretches to go exploring. I suppose it is a bit like Michael's father, traveling far away. But it doesn't bother me, because I'm not used to having my father around. My brothers and I sleep in this very holly tree so we can be near Mother.

I try to help Mother repair the nest, telling her more about the boy. "I don't like him," I say. "He banged on the glass at me."

"What!" Mother looks alarmed. I'm immediately sorry I mentioned it. "I hope he isn't that kind of boy, Mirabelle. You have to be careful. Remember what happened to Aunt Aurelia."

This is a story my brothers and I have heard many times. It happened before we were born, but it's part of the family lore. One day, Aunt Aurelia landed on the old man's bird feeder, the one by the kitchen window, and as she was munching away—sunflower seeds, delicious—the younger brother of one of the piano students ran up to the window and banged on it. Aunt Aurelia was so startled that she flapped into the air without looking, and she flew straight into the hedge where the old man's cat was hiding.

It was a terrible way to go.

"I remember," I say.

"Well, I certainly hope so," Mother says. "Would you like to do something for me? Take Sebastian and Oliver and fetch some spiderwebs. I need them to finish the nest."

Spiderwebs—or caterpillar silk, when we can find it—are a good addition to the nest because they make everything stick together. I know my brothers will be delighted with this assignment. They think it's fun to scare the big brown spider that lives in the eaves of the garden shed. I, on the other hand, always feel bad about taking away part of her web, since we're destroying something she made just to make something of our own. That doesn't seem fair, does it? But Mother tells me not to worry; a spider can spin a web in a day.

Still, that spider is never happy to see us.

Where are my brothers? I fly over the holly tree, scanning the old man's green, shrubby backyard for anything small and yellow.

And there they are, in the birdbath, having a water fight. Sebastian is flapping through the water, drenching Oliver, who's making a desperate, strangled chirping noise in protest.

I swoop down, close enough to get their attention but not so close that they can spray me with water. "Hey!" I call. "Mother needs some spiderweb for the nest."

"Yay!" says Sebastian, flying up to join me.

Oliver is too wet, though. He has to sit on the edge of the bird-bath and flutter his wings to dry off.

"Wait," he whines. "Don't go without me!"

So Sebastian and I fly in circles above him until he's fluffed his feathers dry.

"I'll get the spider's attention," Sebastian offers.

"No, I will," says Oliver, and they start to argue over it.

I am not about to volunteer for this job. We need the spider out of the web so we can take as much of it as we want, but she is a big spider, with a bulging, hairy brown body, and even though she's scared of us, truth be told, I am scared of her, too. First of all, she BITES. I have never been bitten, but it is supposed to really, really hurt. Second of all, unlike lots of birds, we goldfinches are mostly vegetarian. We hardly ever eat insects except by accident. And one of the problems with the spider's web is that all sorts of little bugs fly into it. Once—I don't even like to talk about this—a *gnat* flew into my mouth! Yuck! I clamped shut my beak, but it was too late. I had already swallowed the horrible little thing. It was disgusting, like eating dirt. And Sebastian and Oliver just laughed and laughed, as if watching me swallow a bug was the funniest thing ever. Since then, it makes me nervous to be around spiderwebs. I am perfectly happy to let one of my brothers get the spider's attention.

Oliver insists that he'll do it, and that Sebastian owes him because Sebastian didn't play fair at the birdbath. This is likely true; Sebastian is a bit of a cheat. He grouses but finally agrees, probably because he feels guilty. The argument ends and we all fly over to the garden shed.

It is a little wooden building with one window and a peaked roof. The old man keeps rakes and shovels here, along with topsoil and mulch, and his noisy lawn mower. The shed smells earthy and warm from the sun. There is a wisteria vine climbing up one side of it, and the pale purple blooms droop in the late June heat.

Sebastian and I settle on the roof, far above the spiderweb. If we crane our necks, we can see the spider, huddled near the center of the web.

Oliver flies in innocent circles overhead. Then, without warning, he dive-bombs toward the web. He comes at it so fast, at such a precise and dastardly angle, that the spider shrinks back in surprise. At the last minute, Oliver swoops upward, but before the spider can recover, he dives again, straight at her. This time, she scurries up under the eaves, abandoning the silvery scaffolding of her web. It glistens in the afternoon light.

"Quick!" says Sebastian.

Together, he and I flap down to the web and start pecking at it, breaking the wet, sticky strands and grabbing the bulk of it in our beaks.

"Look out!" calls Oliver.

Uh-oh. That bulbous brown spider is creeping out from under the eaves, coming to protect her web.

She is so close that I can see the long, wiry hairs on her legs.

Yikes!

My mouth is full of spiderweb, so I can't speak, but I nod quickly at Sebastian, and he nods back at me.

Just as the spider crawls toward us, we flutter up in tandem, with the web slung between us like a hammock.

We leave that spider behind with nothing but a few tattered strands of her beautiful handiwork, blowing in the breeze.

Oliver leads the way back to the nest. It is tricky to negotiate our path through the sharp holly leaves without losing pieces of the precious web.

"Oh, wonderful," Mother says when she sees us. "You're just in time. Here, help me lay it along this wall."

Sebastian and I drop the web over the curved wall of grass and vines. Mother plucks the slender filaments with her beak and gently spreads them over the nest.

"There," she says. "That's just perfect, much stronger than before. I won't have to worry about thunderstorms now."

My brothers and I gather to admire her craftsmanship. Mother always makes things nice and cozy. I can see that she's added more thistledown, to create a comfy blanket of fluff where she'll lay her eggs.

Sebastian, Oliver, and I perch on a nearby branch, settling in for the evening. I'm still thinking about the boy. When will I get to hear him play? Will he be as good as everyone seems to think he is? And why did he tell me to go away?

You'd think he would appreciate having a bird for an audience, especially one as musically advanced as myself. I make up my mind to watch his next lesson, but this time he won't see me at all.

4

Emily

Well, I can tell you are dying to know: Is the boy any good? Can he really *play*? Unfortunately, I have no idea. Because here is what happens with the boy and the piano: lesson after lesson after lesson, he refuses to play.

He comes three times the first week, and the old man brings out new sheet music and even plays for him—Bach and Brahms and Debussy, lovely, haunting notes that ripple together like a crystalline mountain stream, sweeping over rocks and into lush pastures. And then Mr. Starek plays Chopin, and I am overcome.

I can hear immediately how Chopin is different—more complicated somehow, a flurry of notes, with a depth and richness like singing. How can that be? These notes on a piano sound like a voice...the most beautiful, intricate voice I've ever heard.

I stay hidden in the silk tree, but oh my goodness, the music enchants me.

Do you think that boy says one nice word of appreciation? Nope. I want to flap some sense into him! Doesn't he know how lucky he is? He has the old man for his teacher, the old man who is gifted and brilliant, who doesn't even teach anymore, despite the long line of students who would give anything to study with him. And here is this boy—this bad-tempered, lazy boy—just taking up space in the music room and not playing anything.

I retreat to the thickest cluster of blossoms, on a high branch of the silk tree. Am I imagining that the boy sometimes looks for me? The first time he came back, he stood at the window for a few minutes, peering out, but he didn't see me. Now he occasionally glances my way, but he never approaches the glass.

Toward the end of the fourth lesson, the boy's mother, Mrs. Jin, arrives early. I hear her talking to the old man on the front porch while the boy is still inside.

"Should we just give up?" she asks, her voice weary. "Michael is very stubborn. He won't play unless he wants to, and he's angry about a lot of things these days. The competition is only eight weeks away! I don't see how he can be ready in time."

The old man nods. "It would be a challenge even if he committed to practicing. But if he won't play..." His voice trails off.

Mrs. Jin sighs. "It would give him so many opportunities if he

28

could excel in front of those judges. A different level of instruction, scholarships, music schools that might be interested in him. Not to mention the prize money, of course. Ten thousand dollars!" She is silent for a minute, lips pursed. "I played myself as a child, but I never had the talent Michael has. I couldn't even dream of playing the way he does. It's so hard to see him squander it."

Mr. Starek looks at her sympathetically. "The festival would open doors for him, there is no question. But I can't force him to play, and there's little point in you continuing to bring him if he refuses." He pauses. "I had a thought: perhaps Emily would be willing to meet us here for his next lesson? She might have better luck changing his mind than you or I."

Mrs. Jin's face brightens. "Oh, do you think she would? I'll call her. It can't hurt. I've tried everything else. He doesn't care that I'm frustrated with him, he doesn't care if I punish him. He's so strong-willed."

The old man smiles. "A strong will is a beautiful thing when it's put to a good purpose. Let's help him find that purpose."

Mrs. Jin shakes her head. "You're very patient, Mr. Starek. I hope we aren't wasting your time."

"Not at all. It has become quite a puzzle, hasn't it? I am eager to hear Michael play."

"Well, after this long wait, I hope you'll find it worth it." The boy's mother opens the front door and calls, "Michael! Please get your things. It's time to go."

So that is how I meet Emily. She comes to the very next lesson. From the moment she steps out of her car, I can't take my eyes off her.

She is as slight as the boy, though taller, with bright, sparkling brown eyes and fine, sharp features. She has reddish-brown hair that curls near her ears and at the back of her neck, like a ruffle of downy feathers. A leather backpack hangs over her shoulder, and she is dressed plainly in jeans and a T-shirt, but she moves so gracefully I am riveted. Oh, she is *something*. I hate to admit it, but even without hearing her play a note, I can see why the boy is so stuck on her.

Michael is already in the house when she arrives, but he must be able to see her car in the driveway because he runs straight out, leaping down the steps and flinging himself at her. I'm afraid he'll knock her over. But she laughs and catches him and spins around, even though she's not that much bigger than he is. "Michael!"

He wraps his arms around her so enthusiastically, it touches my heart. I haven't seen him this excited about anything, certainly not the lessons.

Mr. Starek comes to the door

and watches the scene in the driveway, smiling. "Emily Gold-berg," he says. "It is wonderful to see you again."

She comes toward him, seeming a little shy. "You too, Mr. Starek. I think the last time was at the Berklee College of Music, wasn't it? You played Rachmaninoff's Fourth. You were AMAZING."

"Ah, I remember that concert. How are you? You're finishing up at the conservatory?"

"Yes, I'm a senior. Music history major."

"Really?" Mr. Starek sounds surprised. "Not piano?"

"No..." Emily's brow furrows. "I love it, but I ended up on the research end of things. I'm actually taking a summer course entirely on Chopin." She hesitates, and her gaze drops shyly. "My senior essay is on Chopin and his muses."

Michael looks from one to the other. "What's a muse?" he asks. I am wondering the same thing.

"Something that inspires you," Emily tells him. "For artists or musicians, the person or thing that helps them do their best work."

Well! Doesn't that sound marvelous? I want a muse.

"How fascinating." Mr. Starek's smile is warm. "You will have to tell me more about your essay. Please come in. I'm hoping you can have a word with Michael here and persuade him to play."

Michael frowns, looking away. He doesn't say anything. Emily loops her arm lightly over his shoulder.

"I hope so, too," she says. "It sounds like he hasn't really started his lessons with you yet."

31

Into the house they go, and I fly quickly to my pink silk tree. I'm about to hide in the blossoms on a high branch, where they can't see me, but I'm dying to watch what's going to happen. So I take a chance and perch on a lower limb—but not close to the window. It's open a few inches, as usual, to let the fresh summer air flow through the screen.

"Here we are," the old man is saying, leading them into the music room. "You remember it, I'm sure, from your high school lessons."

"Oh, yes," Emily says. "This Érard is so beautiful." She rests one hand on the glossy top of the piano so gently she might be touching glass. She turns to Michael. "It's one of Chopin's pianos," she tells him.

Michael's eyes widen. "It is? Really?" he asks, suddenly riveted. I am startled to see the grouchiness fall away from him as easily as molting feathers.

Emily laughs. "Wait, I don't mean his actual piano."

Mr. Starek is smiling, too. "Those are in museums! The ones that been found, at least."

Michael looks curious, finally. "What do you mean?" he asks. "Were they lost?"

I am bewildered by this, too. How do you lose a piano?

But Emily is still talking about the Érard. "It's not Chopin's own piano. It's just one of the two kinds he liked to play," she continues. She turns to Mr. Starek. "Michael loves pianos, almost as much as he loves playing them."

32

The old man raises his eyebrows. "Do you, Michael? I wish you could have met my sister, Halina. She loved pianos, too. She was a great...collector of musical things."

We all wait for him to go on. I only know Halina through the old man's sadness at her death. But he has been so sad for so long, I am sure that there was something very special about her. Feelings can be almost mathematical like that, don't you think? When you lose something, your sadness is exactly equal to how much you cherished it.

Mr. Starek's expression clouds. "She was a collector of too many things."

Michael looks at the old man and I can see from his face that his obstinance is battling with interest.

Emily is also surprised. "I didn't know you had a sister," she says. "Did she live in Poland?"

"No, no," Mr. Starek answers hurriedly, and it's clear that he wants the conversation to end. "She lives...she lived a few miles from here, over the bridge. We had not spoken in many years."

"Oh." Emily clearly doesn't know what to say. The room is awkwardly quiet. I almost want to tap on the window myself to break the tension.

"Please." The old man gestures to Emily. "Let me hear you play."

Emily slips onto the bench, lifting the lid. Her long, pale fingers brush the keys for a moment, and then, abruptly, she begins.

The air fills with the delicate chimes of some piece I've never heard before. I know instantly it must be Chopin. Oh, she plays so prettily! Her touch is quick and light, and she sways forward on the bench as her fingers dart over the keys. Her face tightens with concentration, her arms spread like wings. The notes trill and merge. I hop down the branch, straining to pick out each sparkling plink.

But here's what I hate to admit, because I want for it not to be true: the music is spectacular, but Emily's playing is not.

As beautiful and polished as it is, the way Emily plays reminds me of the second kind of student the old man has taught, the one who tries so hard. She has the technical ability—look how fast her fingers fly!—but what she lacks, in the end, is *art*.

Part of me is crestfallen because I wanted so badly for her to be great. I did! I know you're thinking, *But you just met her—why would you care?* I can't explain it. I think I am a little in love with her already. There is something about her—the way she carries herself, her quick grace—that is very birdlike. I wanted her to have a bird's ease with music. I wanted it to pour out naturally.

I can tell that the old man feels the same way I do. Emily glances up at him when she finishes, her face flushed and full of hope.

He smiles and says, "That was delightful."

She says "Thanks," but I can see her shoulders slump. "I couldn't really compete at the conservatory. That's why I'm doing music history." Then she brightens. "I mean, it's good—I like my major. I love the research."

"Well, you're still an excellent pianist," Mr. Starek says

warmly. "And that piece was a fine choice." He turns to Michael. "Did you recognize it?"

Michael doesn't say anything.

Ugh, the boy isn't even polite. My mother would certainly not approve of the way he treats the old man. He's a guest in Mr. Starek's house, a pupil of this revered piano teacher, yet he acts like he'd rather be anywhere but here.

"You know it," Emily tells him. "Chopin, the Polonaise in A major. Do you want to try?"

Michael shakes his head again.

"Oh, Michael, come on." Emily sounds exasperated.

The old man studies the two of them. "Please excuse me for a moment," he says. "There's something I need to attend to."

When he leaves, they are alone in the music room, the birdlike girl and the stubborn boy. I dig my claws into the branch of the silk tree and cock my head, listening for whatever comes next.

"You need to play, Michael," Emily says. "It's been two weeks since our last lesson. You were so excited about the festival! What happened?"

Michael shrugs and stomps over to the window. I'm afraid he's going to see me, so I duck quickly behind the blossoms, and then I freeze. He seems to be staring right at me, but he doesn't bang on the window or utter a word.

Emily stands. "I know you can play anything, but you still need to prepare. You'll never be ready in time if you don't start practicing."

Michael isn't looking at her. He still seems to be looking at *me*.

"Mr. Starek can take you to a whole new level," Emily pleads. "Why won't you play for him?"

The boy glares through the window with his dark, angry eyes.

"Listen to me." Emily bends slightly, her face close to his. "Do you know what? It would take me months—years maybe—to learn these pieces you play perfectly."

Michael finally turns toward her, and I see his expression change.

She continues, her voice low and fierce. "If I studied the piano for the rest of my life, if I played every single day, all day long, I would never be as good as you are right now."

This unsettles me so much that I rock the branch, and the pink flowers rustle. I hear the longing in her voice, and the certainty, and the sadness.

For the first time, I wonder what it would be like to really, really love something that you knew you would never be great at.

I think about how much I love to sing. Would I love it as much if I couldn't sing well? I want to believe I would. But honestly, I don't know.

Is that why Emily's a piano teacher? To find in somebody else the talent she lacks? It must be heartbreaking, to spend your days pressing hard against the wall of your own limits, everything you wish you could do, everything you wish you were.

I think about the sheer luck of having a gift. The boy has a gift, apparently. Is he really so good? Will I ever find out? Right on the wings of that thought comes this other one: How do you truly know if you have a gift? I mean, it fills me with joy to sing, but what if the passion itself isn't enough? Who's to say what genius really is? Maybe it is something that you can never know about yourself, something that only other people can judge.

It's not as if there's a flock of birds telling me my songs are more exquisite than any they've ever heard.

Oh, but I *want* for them to be!

I don't like the way all of this is making me feel. There's a sickening pit in my stomach, like the time I ate that gnat. I want to fly home to the holly tree. I'm on the verge of doing just that when Michael speaks.

"I don't want to play for him. I want to play for you."

Emily straightens and now she looks mad. "You shouldn't be playing for him or for me! You should play for yourself."

Michael recoils. I can tell he's not used to seeing her temper.

But she touches his arm and leads him to the piano.

"Just sit here with me," she says, softening. "And I will tell you some interesting things about this piano."

5

Lost Pianos

Michael slides onto the piano bench next to her. "What?"

Emily strokes the keys lightly. "They've been making this type of piano since the early 1800s. Think how long ago that is! Chopin was very fussy about what kind of piano he played. He had two he liked, and the Érard was one of them. Do you want to hear what he had to say about it?"

"Okay," Michael says. He is staring at the piano.

"Wait, I'll read his exact words," Emily says. "It's in my notebook from class." She leans over to grab her backpack and pulls out a blue spiral notebook.

"What class? It's summer," Michael protests.

"I'm taking a summer course on Chopin. Here, listen." She

thumbs through the thin pages, then reads, "'When I am not in the mood, I play on the Érard piano, where I find the ready tone easily.'"

Michael looks puzzled. "What does that mean?"

"It means that even the greatest musicians sometimes don't feel like playing," Emily tells him. "But they still do it. And the Érard—this piano—is the perfect one to play when you're not in the mood."

"Why?" Michael asks. "Why is it good for that?"

"It has a beautiful tone. Listen."

She plays Chopin's polonaise again, just a few bars, her fingers dancing. The room fills with the piano's strong, clear, pure notes.

She turns to Michael. "It sounds different from a regular piano, right?"

Now, I have to confess, this is the only piano I've ever heard, because I've only ever heard piano music at Mr. Starek's house. But Michael must agree with her, because he is nodding.

"If this is what Chopin played when he wasn't in the mood," he asks slowly, "what kind of piano did he play when he *was* in the mood?"

Good question, right? The boy is smart, I have to give him that.

Emily smiles at him. "I knew you were going to ask that." She opens her notebook again. "It's part of the same quote." She reads, "'But when I am full of vigor and strong enough to find my very own tone—I need a Pleyel piano.'"

Michael leans over her lap, reading along with her. "Play-el," he pronounces carefully.

"Yes," Emily says. "It was Chopin's absolute favorite kind of piano. He had many Pleyels during his life, because he was

good friends with the guy who made them. He composed his most famous works on them. Seven of his Pleyels are in museums or private collections."

"Really? Pianos that Chopin actually played on?" Michael asks, his face eager, and I can see

what Emily said is true: this boy loves pianos. "Where are they?"

"There's one in France," Emily says. "And I think Poland and Sweden. And I know a Pleyel that belonged to Chopin was recently discovered in a house in Germany." She shakes her head. "Can you imagine how those people felt, when they realized they owned a piano that was once played by Chopin?"

We are all quiet, thinking about that: the amazing luck of it, the wonder.

"That would be *crazy*," Michael says reverently. "Playing a piano he actually played." He pauses. "What about the others? You said there were more."

Emily nods. "About twenty, I think. Chopin's lost pianos. The others have never been found."

Again, I think, A lost piano? Who ever heard of such a thing? A piano is too big to lose.

"How did they get lost?" Michael asks. "Aren't they worth a lot of money?"

"Oh, sure," Emily says. "They'd each be worth a fortune, millions, if anyone could find one and know for certain that it belonged to Chopin. You'd need proof that it was his."

What would that be? I wonder. Do people put their names on their pianos? I doubt it.

"Why did he have so many?" Michael asks. "We only have one piano at my house."

"Because of his friend Camille Pleyel, who owned a piano-making company. He gave Chopin a new one every year, sometimes more often. Chopin taught piano lessons, like Mr. Starek does—like I do—and I guess Pleyels have such an unusual tone that once you play on one, you never want to play anything else. So Chopin's piano students would often buy a Pleyel piano after learning to play on it. It was good advertising for the company to supply Chopin with new pianos."

Michael is mesmerized. "What makes Pleyels so different?"

Emily pauses. "I've never played one. Mr. Starek could tell you."

Michael stares at the Érard. "And now nobody knows where they are? Chopin's pianos?"

"They ended up scattered all over the world," Emily says. "They were sold to other musicians, passed down as family treasures. I remember reading that some of those French Pleyels even got shipped here, to America. But it's hard to trace their owners over the course of two hundred years. My professor said there was a rumor that a Chopin piano had been discovered in Canada a while ago. It was so exciting! But it just turned out to be a Pleyel from the same time period, not one of his."

Emily rises from the piano bench and tucks her notebook into her bag.

"Why don't you try playing?" she suggests. "I know you don't want to. But remember, Chopin played on a piano just like this one when *he* didn't want to. And if Chopin could do it, so can you."

Michael looks at her, then back at the piano. "I wish it was a Pleyel."

"Me too! But you've never played on an Érard," she coaxes. "It will be like traveling back in time. And over the ocean! To Paris in the 1800s."

Oh, this Emily is a dreamer, I can tell. I think she and I could be good friends, don't you? The boy doesn't say anything. *Quit*

42

stalling, Michael, I long to shout at him. *Don't you want to travel back in time?*

When Michael still doesn't answer, she says, "Come on, play something easy. What about the Minute Waltz? I'm going to talk to Mr. Starek."

She leaves the room, closing the door behind her.

6

Duet

So here we are again: the boy, the piano, and me.

Michael stands near the piano, just looking at it. I can tell you, I am not expecting much. There have been too many days of him doing exactly this, nothing else.

But then he walks to the door and listens for a minute. I listen, too. Distantly, I can hear Emily's voice intertwining with Mr. Starek's deeper one, but I can't tell what they're saying. Of course, I could fly around to the kitchen window and really hear their conversation, but I don't want to leave the boy.

I am watching him closely.

Something changes.

Michael sits down at the piano bench.

Even his posture is different: his back straight, his head alert. He lifts his hands and positions them over the keys. I see his long fingers, the graceful curve of his wrists. He leans toward the piano, his face tense, his dark hair flopping over his forehead.

Is he really going to play? After all this time?

I hold my breath.

When the music starts, it comes in a torrent, a rush of silvery notes cascading over one another. Instantly, three things are clear to me:

I have never heard playing like this before.

I don't want it to ever end.

And I have to—I just have to—SING.

What pours out of me then is a stream of notes I don't even recognize. They are as fast and bright and pure as the chiming of bells. It's as if the song is singing *me*.

I can feel my head open up like a door, and something I didn't even know existed soars out, coursing through the air, leaping and spinning, dancing with the music the boy is making.

And the boy hears!

His eyes were closed but now he turns to the window. He doesn't stop playing. He looks at me, and his whole face glows with awe.

The singing and the music weave and braid, and they become something else entirely, a third thing filling the air between us.

Michael laughs with joy, and he plays faster, fingers flying, cheeks flushed, bending over the keys, then turning to watch me sing.

I couldn't stop now if I tried.

I sing and sing.

Am I still made of bones and skin and feathers?

No.

I am only song.

He plays, I sing, he plays, I sing, the singing and playing seem bound to last forever.

But then, with a final tinkling rush, the Minute Waltz ends.

The last piano notes ring through the air, and the strange magic that has possessed us fades away.

Michael is just a boy at a piano. I am just a bird on a branch.

The door to the music room swings open.

Emily and Mr. Starek are gazing at Michael in astonishment.

"What *was* that?" Emily cries.

Mr. Starek's face is as rapt and lit as if he has heard the music of angels. "Oh, my boy," he says. "You can *play*."

The Secret

So that's how it begins. I have never sung this way in my entire life, this flurry of notes, in a melody that isn't even mine. I am singing Chopin! It's as if I have a tiny piano inside my head.

And I can tell the boy has never played this way. He is as amazed by it as I am.

As soon as Mr. Starek and Emily come into the room, I start to worry that they heard my singing through the closed door. What if they demand to know where that miraculous sound came from, that beautiful, impossible, piano-like voice? And if they do, can I resist taking the credit?

Honestly, I don't know, but I never get to find out, because it quickly becomes clear that they didn't hear me at all. Now, as

I told you, birds have much better ears than humans do, even though ours are hidden. Apparently, through the thick wooden door of the music room, all Mr. Starek and Emily heard was Michael, and his playing took their breath away.

At first, I do wish they could appreciate my singing—I want an audience so badly!—but I realize that would create a whole bunch of problems. And besides, someone did appreciate it: Michael.

At the end of the lesson, when Mrs. Jin arrives, and Mr. Starek and Emily go outside to tell her what's happened, Michael and I are alone again for a minute. He comes to the window and looks right at me. His eyes are shining. He touches the screen and whispers, "That was awesome. It's like you have a little piano inside you."

Yes! I want to shout. That's what it feels like to me, too.

"I've never played the Minute Waltz that fast before!" he says. "It was magic—I played it fast without even trying. You have to come back, bird. I want to do it again."

Of course I'll come back! I want to do it again, too.

When I fly into the holly tree late that afternoon, Mother can tell something's up. "Why, Mirabelle," she says. "What have you been doing? You are positively glowing."

Sebastian snorts. "She may be glowing but she'll never be as bright a yellow as we are—right, Mother?"

"That's not what I mean," Mother says, waiting for me to answer.

For a second, I consider singing the new song I've learned, Chopin's Minute Waltz. I know it would blow them away. Haha, blow them away—that's a good one for birds. But I'm worried that Mother won't like me singing with the boy. She'll think it's too dangerous, exposing myself that way to the human world.

Of course, I've sung for Mr. Starek before, but only birdsong, not *Chopin*. Who would believe I could do this, sing note after note of the finest, most beautiful piano music ever heard? Nobody knows about my talent. Only the boy's talent.

And what talent! There is something about the way he plays that purely thrills me. The music feels *alive*, with its own beating heart.

Mother is still looking at me expectantly, and I realize I haven't answered her question. "Well, Mirabelle? What have you been doing that's made you so happy today?"

I say carefully, "That boy started to play the piano. And guess what, he's really good. Actually, he's amazing."

"Is he? Well, that must be nice for the old man, to finally have a pupil worthy of him."

"Yes," I say, "he was very pleased."

This seems enough information to satisfy Mother. "Good," she says. "He deserves some happiness after all the sadness he's had lately, with his sister dying. And his worries about her house."

We don't really understand the trouble with Halina's house,

50

except that the old man keeps having tense phone conversations in the kitchen with people from the bank. He's sometimes so pre-occupied, he forgets to fill the bird feeder. From what I can tell, his sister owed a lot of money to the bank, and the old man has to figure out a way to pay it. We birds don't really understand human money, because we don't have anything similar. We give each other gifts once in a while—crows especially love to give gifts—but we never pay anybody anything.

"I think the boy's playing will cheer him up," I tell Mother.

"I do hope so," she says.

I wait a second, then ask casually, "So is it okay for me to watch the music lessons?"

This is a ploy my brothers and I use when there's something we'd like to do that Mother might not approve of. We ask for permission to do a more ordinary thing, and then go a bit further on our own.

"Are you being careful not to get too close to the window?" Mother asks.

"Yes, Mother," I say dutifully.

"Then I suppose it's all right. Listening to such fine music must be doing you good."

Sebastian rolls his eyes. "Come on," he says to me. "There's still time for Flight Club before it gets dark."

Flight Club is a game that Sebastian, Oliver, and I play where one of us is the leader and executes a series of daring dives and turns in midair, and the other two have to follow. If one of the followers is able to do all the maneuvers and fly ahead of the leader, then that bird becomes the leader. It is a fun game. But right now, all I can think about is singing Chopin.

"I'm a little tired," I say.

"From what?" Ollie demands. "All you've done today is sit on a branch and watch a piano lesson."

Uh-oh, it's enough trouble to keep Mother from getting suspicious. My brothers will be harder to fool.

"Okay," I relent. "Let's play."

And so we play Flight Club until the sun sets, and Sebastian wins, as usual.

I am so excited for Michael's next lesson, and incredibly, I don't have long to wait. The boy shows up the very next day. It is Emily who brings him, not his mother, which confuses me at first—though of course I am delighted to see Emily. Apparently, Mrs. Jin has decided that Emily was such a positive influence on the last lesson that she has hired her to drive Michael to Mr. Starek's house in the afternoons—and it seems that Emily is very pleased with the arrangement.

"I can do my homework while I'm here," Emily says to Mr. Starek. "If it's okay with you, I mean. And maybe I can watch

Michael's lessons sometimes. I love hearing him play, and I'd like to see how you teach him."

"Of course it's okay," Mr. Starek says. "You are more than welcome."

What a good idea, I think, since Emily teaches piano herself. I'm sure she can learn a lot from Mr. Starek, and I'm just happy I'll get to see her more often.

Michael rushes past her into the music room. "Where's the yellow bird that's always here?" he cries.

"Ah, the pretty little goldfinch?" Mr. Starek asks, and I feel a swell of pride. The old man remembers me!

But then I realize I have something else to worry about. Is Michael going to tell them about my singing?

It occurred to me yesterday that he might tell them about me, might point to my perch and blurt it all out. But in their flurry of excitement and gush of compliments, Michael never once mentioned my singing. He did glance my way a couple of times—excited, secret looks—but he didn't say anything about us making music together.

Why not? Did he realize it would be unsafe to tell Mr. Starek and Emily?

I know what my mother would say. She's told me about birds who sing pretty songs for humans, and birds who learn human speech...canaries, nightingales, parrots. "Humans will catch you and put you in a cage! People love having birds perform for their entertainment. Is that the life you want?"

No! No, it is not. The very thought terrifies me. A cage?! What if I could no longer soar over the fields or eat my nutty sunflower seeds? What if I couldn't splash in the birdbath with Sebastian and Oliver? That would be an awful life for a goldfinch, trapped in a cage in somebody's living room.

So it has to stay a secret, my singing with the piano. That is very hard for me, because the music is so beautiful, all I want is for everyone to hear it…Mr. Starek and Emily, and most especially Mother. Why, Mother would love this! She would be so proud.

But that can't happen. And the boy must know it, too. He says nothing about my singing. Does he think that Mr. Starek or Emily would put me in a cage?

They don't seem like they would, but you never know. Humans will engage in all sorts of foolishness when they really want something. And I can certainly imagine they would want to hear more of my singing.

Whatever his reasons, Michael doesn't tell them, and I know better than to sing in front of them. So it remains our secret.

He looks for me as soon as he enters the music room. I make sure I'm easy to see, perched on a branch by the window, but not too close. This time, I hang from the branch upside down. We goldfinches are good at that. We are tiny gymnasts. We can hold on to anything, from any angle.

Is it going to happen again? Our duet? This is what I haven't stopped thinking about for the last twenty-four hours. What if it was just that once, a fleeting miracle, and now the boy is going to practice the piano as usual, with Mr. Starek at his side?

Oh, I can't stand it! I want to sing with him again.

So I am waiting, upside down, on the branch, with my heart in my throat. I really don't know what will happen.

The boy grins at me and turns to the old man, a little nervously. "Mr. Starek?" he asks, and he seems so different now: careful, polite. "Is it okay if I play by myself first? Just to warm up? It gets me ready to practice."

I feel a surge of joy.

"Of course," Mr. Starek says. "That kind of individual preparation is very important—and it's clearly helping you achieve the 'singing tone' that Chopin aimed for at the piano. Truly, Michael, I've rarely heard it come through as beautifully as when you played yesterday."

A singing tone! Well, what do you think of that? No wonder this music seems made for me.

"Emily." Mr. Starek beckons to her. "Why don't you join me in the kitchen for a few minutes?"

Emily swings her backpack by the strap and says, "Sure. I can start my homework."

Then they leave, closing the door with a soft click.

As soon as we're alone, Michael sits at the piano and looks right at me.

"Let's try a polonaise," he says.

And just like that, we begin again. The music floats through the air, warbling and singing and wrapping around me, and my voice joins it, a river of gorgeous, shimmering notes.

8

Names

So this is what we do, lesson after lesson. And the music...oh, the music! Waltzes and polonaises, études and nocturnes. I like just the sound of the names. Each piece is more lovely than the last, delicate and frilly and complicated, like the lace of Mr. Starek's dining room tablecloth. Mr. Starek calls Chopin "a poet of the piano," and now that I am singing his music, I can see why. Each note seems so carefully chosen. Together, they create an ocean of feeling.

As soon as the door to the music room closes and Michael and I are alone, I sing and sing. I never knew my voice could do this, the loops and twirls and pirouettes. It's as if the music has been buried inside me all along, just waiting for this moment to rush into the world.

Each time Michael arrives for a lesson, he looks out the window to find me. Even if it's raining, I show up...because, you see, that is the first requirement for the true artist: you have to show up! To practice. To perform. To create.

"Hi, bird," Michael will say, with a big grin on his face. "What do you feel like today? That nocturne we tried last time? I've been working on it at home."

He talks to me like we're partners. And then he puts the sheet music for Nocturne number twenty on the music rack, and begins to play.

And I want to sing so badly I cannot contain myself. I feel the song welling inside me.

Now, the nocturnes are hard for me, I'm not going to lie. They start out slowly, one note at a time, and birdsong is never slow! It is impossible for me to sing slowly. So for the nocturnes, I have two choices: I can either harmonize softly while Michael plays the slow part, or I can wait a bit and then join in when the rippling cascade of notes begins.

Michael seems to understand this, because he never looks surprised when I don't jump in immediately. But when my song bursts forth, I see a smile flash across his face and it seems that his fingers move even more quickly and lightly over the keys. And that, in turn, only makes the song rise up in me, with all its beautiful twists and turns, to weave and flow and dance with his playing.

It's like a competition between the two of us! Except that we're both winning. And as the song and the music come together, the boy and I make something entirely new.

One day near the end of the lesson, we hear the clang of the bell on the front porch, signaling the arrival of Mrs. Jin, and Mr. Starek says, "I need to discuss the festival program with your mother, Michael. It will just take a few minutes." As he leaves to answer the door, Emily notices me.

"Hey," she says. "There's that pretty bird."

Oops! I usually try to stay hidden behind the silk blossoms, but I had hopped down the branch to better hear what they were talking about. Well, at least she thinks I'm pretty. I mean, of course I *am* pretty, but it's always nice when humans notice that. I preen a little, for her benefit, smoothing my feathers with my beak.

"He's always there," Michael tells her. "He likes to watch me play."

Wait, *what*? HE?

I feel a rising tide of panic. All this time, Michael has taken me for a boy bird! I am horrified. What if that's why he likes me?

But before I have much chance to ponder this, Emily interrupts him.

"*She*. The female goldfinches aren't as bright yellow as the males. That one is definitely a female."

Oh, thank heavens. Of course Emily knows about birds. Emily is wonderful.

"Yeah?" Michael continues to look at me, tilting his head. I tilt my head to match his pose, and he grins.

"I'm going to give her a name," he says.

Yikes. I don't like where this conversation is going. First he thought I was a boy bird, and now he's going to come up with a name for me that is not my name? And I'll have to listen to him calling me that? I am starting to panic all over again.

"What kind of bird did you say she is?" he asks Emily.

"A goldfinch," Emily says.

"Okay, what about Goldie?" he asks.

Is he serious? Come on, Michael, make a little effort. What would he call a bluebird…Blue?

"Goldie," he calls, walking toward the window.

I deliberately turn myself around on the branch and hop away from him, flashing my tail feathers.

"I don't think she likes that name," Emily says.

"What should I call her, then?" Michael asks.

This is my chance. But how can I tell Michael and Emily my name? It seems impossible.

There has to be a way. I rush at the window and flap my wings frantically to get their attention.

"What about Flap?" Michael says.

Oh my heavens, this is going from bad to worse.

Suddenly, I have an idea. The bell! I will show them the bell. At least that's half my name. It wouldn't be the end of the world if Michael started calling me Belle. Better than Goldie...or Flap. Quickly, I fly around the corner of the house to the front door. I'm a little worried that Mrs. Jin will be standing there talking to Mr. Starek, but the porch is empty—and it stays empty because Michael and Emily don't follow me. I guess they just think I've flown away.

Ugh. Back I go to the music room, flying close to the window this time and hovering, the way I do at the bird feeder when it's too crowded to land.

"Look, she's back," Emily says.

"She wants us to follow her," Michael decides.

Good boy!

Now that I'm sure they're watching me, I fly around the corner of the house to the front porch and land in the yew bush, waiting for them.

Their voices carry through the open window.

"Where do you think she went?" Emily asks.

"She flew that way," Michael says. "Let's find her before my mom says I have to go."

They come to the front door and open it, as I had hoped they would. I can hear Mr. Starek and Mrs. Jin talking in the kitchen. I fly out of the bush, in front of them, and then land perfectly—if I do say so myself—on top of the large bell that hangs over the porch.

"Look!" Emily says, pointing at me. "She's right there, on the bell."

"Bell!" Michael says triumphantly. "Let's call her Bell."

Hooray! It's close, and certainly better than the alternatives.

But I have another idea. I fly quickly to the side mirror of Emily's car, which is parked in front of Mrs. Jin's in the driveway. I land on top of it, hold tight with my claws, and tap the mirror with my beak. I can see my face up close in the glass, like another bird looking right at me. I know about mirrors and reflections because Mother is always afraid we'll fly into a window or peck at our reflections thinking it's another bird. I have seen birds do this, and believe me, it looks ridiculous.

"Now she's on your car," Michael says. "Do you think she wants us to call her Car?"

Honestly, for a stunningly gifted piano player, he is not very smart about names.

"No," Emily says, "I don't think so. I think she's tapping the mirror."

As soon as she says that, I rush back to the bell and land on it again. This is becoming exhausting, but they've almost got it.

"Bell. Mirror," Michael says. "Bell-mirror. That's a weird name."

Oh, for heaven's sake. Come on, people.

I fly back to Emily's car, tap the side mirror, and zip over to the bell again.

"What if it's the other way around?" Emily says. "Mirror. Bell. Mirror...bell. Wait! Mirabelle!"

I can't believe it. They got it! They know my name!

I fly in ecstatic loop-the-loops through the air. Then I swoop down and land on a tree branch right above them.

"Mirabelle? Is that right?" Emily asks gently.

"If it is, she should come to us when we call her name," Michael declares. He holds out his finger. "Mirabelle, come here."

Am I really supposed to land on his finger? Mother would have a fit.

I hesitate for a second, thinking that I would be punished for a thousand years if my mother saw me doing this.

But I want so badly for them to know my name.

So I fly swiftly toward Michael and land for a second on his slim finger, gently closing my claws around it.

I have never felt human skin before. It is soft and warm under my feet, but the bone beneath it is hard and straight, as sturdy as a stick.

For an instant, the boy and I are looking right at each other.

Michael's whole face shines with happiness. "Look, Emily! I have a bird on my FINGER! Mirabelle is letting me hold her."

I stay there for one

more second—that's all—and then I take off, fluttering high above them. Too much excitement for one day! It is time to go home.

Now, I know you must be wondering: Am I really becoming friends with this boy? After the way things started out between us? I keep thinking back to the day Michael banged on the window, a few weeks ago…how frightened I was, and how I thought he was the cruel, rough sort of person who did that kind of thing without a second thought.

But now I know he's not.

I think maybe he was just mad that he couldn't take lessons with Emily anymore, so that bad mood spilled over onto everything else that day. He didn't like the old man, he didn't like the lesson, he didn't like ME because I was at the window watching him.

Everyone is allowed to have a bad day once in a while. And it would be terrible if I based my whole opinion of the boy on that one bad day. People (and birds) deserve second chances, don't you think? And now that I know what Michael is capable of, how passionately and thrillingly he plays the piano, I am happy to give him a second chance.

It's funny…when I first met this boy—this bad-tempered, window-banging boy—would I ever have thought I could show myself to him and trust him with my singing? No, no, a hundred times no. But with our first duet, something changed between us.

I feel like we're a team, and I can't wait to see what we do next.

9

A Possible Pleyel

For two weeks, this is how we go on: the private warm-up, where the boy plays and I sing, and then the lesson, where Mr. Starek instructs him. Now, Mr. Starek is not the kind of teacher who yells at his students or bosses them around. He is very gentle—a listener, not a talker. He will sometimes play a piece himself, then have the student play it, while he sits nearby, watching and listening carefully. Afterward, he makes a few comments, says what they did well, says what they need to work on. And then the student usually plays the passages of music where they need the most help, over and over again. With Mr. Starek's regular students, that was always the point in the lesson when I would fly off to the holly tree, because who wants to listen to the same fragment of music again and again? Boring, right?

Somehow, with Michael's lessons, it isn't. I don't know why. Maybe it's because I've been singing Chopin's music, so when Mr. Starek makes corrections or suggestions for Michael's playing, it helps me, too.

"Gently there, then more force with the transition," Mr. Starek will say. "That is the emotional center of the piece."

I listen carefully to his comments, and the next time Michael and I practice together, I know where to put the emotion in my singing. Some of the pieces are sad, some are serious and thoughtful, some are bright and merry. It matters to get the feeling right.

There's another way that Michael's piano lessons aren't like the lessons with Mr. Starek's previous students. Here, we are all working on something together. It's not just Mr. Starek, Michael, and me. Emily is part of it, too. Even if Mrs. Jin comes to pick up Michael herself, so she can talk to Mr. Starek about his progress, Emily stays for the whole lesson. She does homework and talks to Mr. Starek and watches the way he teaches Michael. I begin to understand that learning how to *do* something is different from learning how to *teach* it. Emily tells Mr. Starek she's learning so much from him, tips she can use with her best students.

And on top of all that, I know she loves hearing Michael play as much as I do.

To my brothers' chagrin, I am perched outside the music room more than ever now. The competition is only six weeks away, and Michael has to choose three pieces to perform. I am trying to help, accompanying him as he performs Chopin's nocturnes and preludes and sonatas. Some of these pieces are very difficult, requiring that he stretch his fingers so far apart over the keys, I think they might break! But the boy doesn't complain, or give up. And for me, there is something delightful in the way that he and Emily call me by name.

"Hey, Mirabelle!" Michael says as soon as he sees me.

Or Emily will glimpse me among the clusters of pink silk blossoms and say, "Look, Michael, Mirabelle is watching you."

I was a little worried, after Emily got involved in the name game, that Michael would confide our secret to her. I could picture him saying, *Guess what—Mirabelle sings along when I play! Come listen to her.* And if he told Emily, what would I do? Emily is so lovely and has such excellent taste, it would be a pleasure to sing for her. I would be sorely tempted! But I know in my heart that would be a mistake.

Because even though Emily isn't entirely grown-up, she is too grown-up for this secret. It would mean something different to her than it means to Michael and me. She might want to *do* something about it. It was a big risk to include her in the naming adventure—I know that. But if I hadn't, I might have ended up with the boy calling me Flap.

Anyway, Michael seems to feel the same way I do. He says my

name, and talks about me, but he never tells Emily the reason he warms up alone. And both Mr. Starek and Emily have been so understanding of that, leaving him by himself at the beginning of each lesson, and showing such joy over the way he plays behind the closed door.

"It's your process," Mr. Starek says. "You must honor your process. These habits and rituals are so important to how we create art."

Emily agrees. She tells Michael, "You never used to warm up alone when you took lessons from me—but it's made such a difference in your playing! Honestly, Michael, when I hear you through the door, it sounds like you're playing TWO pianos. It's amazing."

"I wish I could play two pianos," Michael says one day as the lesson is finishing up. "This one, the Érard, and a Pleyel."

Mr. Starek looks surprised. "A Pleyel? Ah...some people think you've never truly experienced Chopin until you've heard it on a Pleyel."

"Does it sound very different?" Michael asks.

Mr. Starek smiles. "It's the piano his music was meant for. It has a more delicate, subtle tone. Chopin's music is not intended to be played loudly. But how do you know about Pleyels?"

"Emily told me," Michael says.

"I saw one once at that museum of historical instruments near Fitchburg," Emily explains.

"The Franklin Collection?" Mr. Starek asks. "That place is marvelous, isn't it?"

"Oh, yes," Emily agrees. "So cool."

Michael's face is flushed and eager. "I want to see one! And I want to play one."

Mr. Starek chuckles. "That would be quite a trick. They're not made anymore. My sister—"

He stops. A shadow clouds his face, as it often does when he talks about Halina. What was the trouble between them? I wonder. Why hadn't he seen her for so many years, when she lived close by the whole time?

"What?" Michael asks.

"Oh, it's not important." Mr. Starek crosses to the window, and I duck behind a cluster of blossoms, not wanting to distract him. "It's probably not even true."

Now Emily looks curious as well, but I can tell she doesn't want to pry.

Michael hesitates, then persists. "What's not true?"

Mr. Starek rubs both hands over his face, sighing. "Years ago, Halina told me she bought a Pleyel piano at an estate sale."

"Wow!" Michael exclaims. "She did? Does she still have it?"

I flinch at his mistake, and Emily worriedly starts to correct him.

But Mr. Starek says quietly, "Halina passed away last winter."

"Oh," Michael says, his shoulders slumping. I can tell he doesn't know what to say. None of us do. The old man looks so sad it breaks my heart.

"As I believe I told you, she was a collector," he continues. "But her collecting became—well, it was an obsession. Her house was filled, top to bottom, with her things. She hadn't let anyone inside for years."

"Not even you?" Emily asks softly.

"Not even me." Mr. Starek gazes out the window, but his eyes are unfocused, unseeing. "And as far as her owning an actual Pleyel, I thought it unlikely. She did have several pianos, I know that. But most of them were worthless."

"Why?" Michael looks disappointed. "If they were old…"

"An old piano is really just a piece of antique furniture," Mr. Starek explains. "Pianos don't age well. They're not like the string instruments—like a Stradivarius violin, for example. Pianos are mechanical, and the mechanics wear out and fail."

"They can be restored, though," Emily says.

"Yes," Mr. Starek agrees. "But generally it's not worth the money to do so. Unless the piano has some other significance."

"Your sister," Emily begins. "Did she restore any of hers?"

Mr. Starek shakes his head. "Oh, no. As I said, nobody was allowed in the house, and the last time I visited…well, it looked like a junkyard." He is still staring through the window, lost in thought. "Halina was so convinced of the value of the things she collected. She was unable to see her acquisitions as…" It seems to pain him to finish the sentence. "A kind of sickness."

Michael looks genuinely bewildered. "But what's sick about that? Lots of people collect things. And she might have a *Pleyel* piano!"

Mr. Starek looks skeptical. "Perhaps."

"Haven't you gone to her house to check?" Michael asks. "What if it's there?"

I can see that Mr. Starek is done with this conversation. "No, I haven't. There's an issue with the bank. Halina took a loan from the bank to pay for the house and she owed a great deal of money when she died, more than the house is even worth. I've been trying to sort that out. And to be honest, I am not sure I am…prepared to see what's in the house."

"I can understand that," Emily says quickly, and she gives Michael a look that says, *Don't ask any more questions.*

Mr. Starek stands at the window in silence, his face a wince of sorrow.

That is my cue. I know how to cheer him up. I hop out from behind the silk blossoms and flutter to the end of the branch, tilting my head at him.

Immediately, his lips curve into a smile. "Here's that charming little goldfinch again," he says. "She must like listening to you play, Michael."

"Oh, she does!" Michael grins. "She's here all the time."

I fly down to the windowsill and alight just for a moment, as close to the screen as I can. But the lesson is over, and it's time for me to head home. As I flap up, up, up into the blue summer sky, I wonder if Sebastian and Oliver have been missing me. I think about Halina, and Mr. Starek not seeing his own sister for years and years, not setting foot in her house. It is so strange and sad. It makes me want to be home, surrounded by my family.

But I also think about the piano. Might there really be a *Pleyel* somewhere in Halina's house? Oh, how wonderful if Michael could play on it! And if I could sing along.

10

At the Bird Feeder

When I get back to the holly tree, Sebastian and Oliver are squabbling over a limp stalk of raspberries.

"Where have you been?" Oliver wants to know, momentarily dropping his end of the stalk.

Sebastian flies away and greedily devours the berries, dark juice streaking his breast. "She just sits around all day by the music room," he tells Oliver with his beak full. "Boring!"

Boring? Oh, he has no idea.

"I'm not sitting around," I protest. "I'm listening to music."

Of course I can't tell them what I'm really doing. They wouldn't understand, and they'd probably make fun of me. Also, I don't want them reporting anything to Mother.

Sebastian rolls his eyes at me. "You can listen to music anytime you want. Just open your mouth."

Before I can answer, Oliver flutters over in a fit of outrage. "Sebastian! You ate all the berries! And I'm starving." He turns to me, peevish. "Why don't you ever do anything with us anymore?"

That makes me feel guilty. "What do you mean? I'll do something with you right now."

"Okay. What?"

"I don't know. What do you want to do?"

We all look at one another blankly. We could ask Mother for an idea, but it would likely involve some chore at the nest.

"The bird feeder!" Oliver cries jubilantly. "The old man just refilled it. Let's get some sunflower seeds."

He flies recklessly in the direction of the bird feeder, and I have to swoop low and fast to catch up to him. Of course Sebastian comes, too, notwithstanding his recent feast of raspberries.

The bird feeder is a small plastic box that sticks to the kitchen window with rubber suction cups. A rounded heap of birdseed, thick with the large black sunflower seeds we love, overflows the rim.

A flashy red cardinal is perched there, but he takes off as soon as we get close. For all their brazen size and color, the boy cardinals are timid. Maybe with good reason: there are three of us.

"Yum!" Oliver says, his good humor restored. "Plenty for everyone!"

He begins to gobble the sunflower seeds, cracking them open

with his beak and scattering a messy shower of dry casings. Sebastian quickly joins in. I land on one side of the feeder and bang a sunflower seed against the hard plastic edge till it splits open, munching the tasty seed inside.

Honestly, they are not as delicious as our favorites, thistle seeds, and they take considerably more work. But they are quite filling. We are diving into this grainy banquet with gusto when we hear a terrible, loud scrabbling against the house's wood siding, and something large and fast launches itself at the feeder.

A squirrel!

ARGH.

Now, believe me, the squirrel has no interest whatsoever in goldfinches; he is all about the birdseed. But his terrifying assault is meant to drive us away, and it most certainly does. His dark paws grip the plastic edge of the feeder and his pushy face looms next to us, and Sebastian, Oliver, and I are so shocked we hurtle down through the air. We

are desperately trying to get out of the way, as the squirrel's giant maw burrows into the birdseed.

It takes us a split second to realize our mistake.

Because there, sitting patiently beneath the feeder, not making a sound, is: the cat.

Awwwk!

Oliver screeches, and the cat vaults skyward, her dagger-sharp claws extended. Sebastian and I turn together, careening toward Oliver and the cat.

"Help me!" Oliver cries as Harmony swipes at his yellow wings and bats him to the ground.

Oliver!

We've got to save him.

We dive toward the cat just as she lunges at Oliver.

Awwwk!

The air is a blur of feathers and fur. I can feel the wet spray of cat spittle, and I see the white glint of Harmony's fangs.

Then, out of nowhere, a streak of gold blazes past us.

Mother!

She flies straight at the cat's head.

"Back to the nest!" she cries, beating her wings fast-fast-fast over Harmony's glowing eyes.

Oliver shoots into the sky, and Sebastian and I quickly follow.

But Mother! All I can think of is poor Aunt Aurelia, caught in that cat's deadly grip.

We circle overhead in terror, watching the fray below. The cat is hurling herself at Mother, swiping the air viciously, and driving Mother toward the bushes, where she'll be unable to escape.

Clap! Clap!

The noise startles all of us, including Harmony. On the deck of the house next door, Mr. Starek's neighbor, Mrs. Garcia, is looking over the fence and clapping her hands loudly. "Harmony, shoo! Leave that bird alone."

Oh, bless her, bless her.

Mother flaps into the air.

Harmony pounces.

My breath stops in my throat.

Bang!

The back door swings open.

"Harmony!" the old man says sharply.

He has a broom in one hand and he whacks the ground near the cat.

That fleeting pause gives Mother the chance she needs to soar toward the roofline, far out of reach.

"Thank you for keeping an eye on things," Mr. Starek says to Mrs. Garcia.

"Of course," Mrs. Garcia calls back to him, laughing. "Poor Harmony. We always ruin her fun."

And as suddenly as it began, the drama is over.

Together, Mother, Sebastian, Oliver, and I fly through the warm summer air, back to the holly tree.

"Wow!" Sebastian crows as soon as we land. "Did you see us? We showed that dumb cat."

"I almost died!" Oliver sobs. "I could see inside her *mouth*."

"What happened?" Mother demands.

"It was the squirrel," I tell her. "We were just having a snack at the bird feeder and a big old squirrel scared us—"

"And Ollie got too close to the cat," Sebastian finishes.

"I did not!" Oliver protests. "We all flew the same way, but she pounced on *me*."

"You should always have a lookout," Mother scolds. "How many times have I told you that? If you're all busy eating, you won't be aware of danger."

It's true, she has told us that. But we forget. And nobody wants to be the lookout when there's a tray full of tasty sunflower seeds to gobble.

Speaking of which, I feel a little sick...bloated from gorging on seeds, and queasy from all that racing around.

"If it hadn't been for us, Ollie wouldn't be here right now," Sebastian announces.

Mother shakes her head. "If it hadn't been for the old man, *I* wouldn't be here right now," she says grimly.

We settle into the prickly holly leaves, thankful to be safe. My heart finally stops pounding.

I'm thinking of the cat, and how ridiculous it is that her name is Harmony. Harmony is something lovely and pleasing, the happy blending of two voices, or two strands of music...like what Michael and I create together. There is nothing harmonious about that awful, bloodthirsty cat.

11

The Heart of Chopin

After the near-death experience at the bird feeder, my ongoing exploits with Michael in the music room seem positively risk-free. There will always be time to play with my brothers; right now Michael and I have important work to do! He still has to choose his three pieces for the festival, which is only five weeks away.

The boy's mother has been bugging him about this. That just seems to be something mothers do, human and bird alike. At the end of one lesson, when Michael is climbing into the car, I hear Mrs. Jin say quietly to Mr. Starek, "I'm so glad he's finally playing for you, but he needs to start focusing on whatever he's going to perform. You saw the list of possibilities for the youth category on the festival website?"

"Yes, I looked them over," Mr. Starek tells her. "I could suggest a few pieces, but it would be better for Michael to choose them himself. I want him to be excited to perform so he doesn't play in a mechanical way."

Mechanical? I couldn't imagine Michael playing anything like a robot. He is so full of feeling when he plays, from the tilt of his head to the flow of his arms.

Mrs. Jin says, "That makes sense. I'm so impressed by Michael's progress. He's playing very differently now, since you started teaching him."

See? Even his mother is pleased with the music we've been making! And while I'm sure Mr. Starek has had a big impact on the way Michael plays, I can't help but think I've had an influence, too.

So that is how the conversation about what to play at the festival gets started. Today Mr. Starek says, "Your playing is coming along so nicely, Michael. And any Chopin piece you play benefits all the other Chopin you play. But we should start preparing for the competition. Have you thought about your three pieces?"

"A little," Michael says.

Emily asks him, "Is there anything you feel particularly excited about?"

"I like the Minute Waltz," Michael says, and my heart leaps, because that was our first duet. "But it's not on the list for the festival."

"No," Mr. Starek says. "And as delightful as it is, it's too straightforward to demonstrate your talents. You need to choose one prelude and one étude for the preliminary rounds."

Michael thinks for a minute. "There's that prelude in D major. The one called 'Tree Full of Songs.'"

Well, isn't that nice? Of course Michael would choose something like that. I haven't sung that piece yet, but I am sure I will be a natural at it. I mean, I've spent my whole life in a tree full of songs.

Mr. Starek nods thoughtfully. "Yes. I like that. It's very short, but a good first piece. What about the études?"

"There's the 'Octaves' one," Emily interjects. "It's so fast, but you have to play it smoothly, which makes it tricky—and it is a stretch for your hands, but you manage that well."

Michael frowns. "I don't like it as much as the one right after, the étude in A minor. It's called 'Winter Wind.'"

Oh, that's the one we were just working on! It really does sound like the wind howling through the bare branches of trees. It's very fast, full of leaps and bangs.

"Good, good," Mr. Starek says. "That's two of the three. The final piece is free choice, but it should be challenging. Maybe one of the sonatas?"

"Oh yes!" Emily cries. "Sonata number three. The second movement is so quick and light. You'll play it beautifully, Michael."

"The scherzo." Mr. Starek nods. "That sonata is considered

one of Chopin's most difficult compositions, and Emily says you already know it."

"Maybe." Michael sounds reluctant.

"The hardest piece will take the most preparation," Mr. Starek says gently. "We should get started soon. Choose something that embodies Chopin, that captures his spirit."

Heavens! That is a lot of pressure.

I can tell Michael thinks so, too, because he turns on the piano bench and plinks two of the keys. "How am I supposed to do that? He's been dead a long time. I don't know what he was like when he was alive."

"Then I will tell you about Chopin," Mr. Starek says. "When you play his music, you must understand who he was. His life, his character, his values."

"Why?" Michael sounds puzzled. "I just play the notes."

"Yes, and you play them very well. But you can only play Chopin's music the way it should be played if you take the time to understand who he was as a person. How his music comes from his personal history."

Michael looks doubtful, so Mr. Starek adds, "That is what will make you stand out from the others at the festival."

The boy is paying closer attention now. I know he wants to win. Not just for the honor of it. Or the prize money—ten thousand dollars!—which Michael has been talking about with great excitement. There are all sorts of opportunities that could come to the boy if he wins—scholarships, and special music schools, and famous piano teachers. Mrs. Jin keeps saying, "It will open doors."

Now, we birds don't like open doors, because sometimes they lead us to fly inside buildings by accident. But humans apparently do like them.

"Mr. Starek's right," Emily chimes in. "Chopin had a really interesting life. It was short—he died at the age of thirty-nine—but he did so much."

"How did he die?" Michael asks.

"Nobody really knows," Mr. Starek says. "Some people say cystic fibrosis, but modern doctors believe he died of complications from tuberculosis. He was ill for most of his life, even as a child."

I'm beginning to get a picture in my mind of this boy, Chopin, pale and sickly, hunched over a piano, making beautiful music.

"He was Polish, like I am," Mr. Starek says. "And even though his father was French and he lived in France much of his life, he always missed Poland. He considered it his true home. That's why he wrote the mazurkas and polonaises."

Those are the merry dancing songs that I've been singing while Michael plays.

"They were inspired by Polish folk music," Mr. Starek says. "So when you play them, you must think of them as love letters to his homeland, the place of his childhood, the place of his heart."

Emily laughs suddenly. "It really is the place of his heart."

Mr. Starek's lips twitch into a small smile. "You know that story?"

"Yes, we talked about it in class." She turns to Michael, explaining, "On his deathbed, it was Chopin's last wish to have his heart returned to Poland. So after he died, the doctor cut it out, and Chopin's sister put it in a crystal jar full of cognac— alcohol—and carried it home. It was placed inside the pillar of a church in Warsaw."

"Really? Just the heart?" Michael looks simultaneously grossed out and fascinated.

I am, too. I have never seen a human heart. I wonder what it looks like. I saw the heart of a squirrel once, run over in the street. It was a tiny, pulpy knot, bright red. It seemed too small to give life to an entire squirrel.

"Just the heart," Emily says. "And there's been such a debate over how Chopin really died that a few years ago, researchers got permission to take the heart out of the pillar and dissect it, just to try to figure out the mystery."

"That's right," Mr. Starek says. "They identified a heart infection linked to tuberculosis in the tissue."

"But the heart would have been so old," Michael says. "How could they tell?"

"The alcohol preserved it," Emily says. "For over a hundred and fifty years! So at least that was one mystery solved."

"One mystery?" Michael looks curious.

Mr. Starek glances at Emily and says, "There are so many mysteries when it comes to Chopin."

"What do you mean?" Michael asks.

I hop down the branch of the silk tree, and peer through the fluff of pink flowers. Is the old man going to tell us a story? I do love a good story.

12

History and Mystery

"What mystery?" Michael asks.

"Well, the mystery of how he died—there's been so much guessing: Was it tuberculosis, was it cystic fibrosis, was it something else entirely?" Mr. Starek says. "But also the mystery of how he possibly survived for so long with whatever sickness plagued him. At that time, people with tuberculosis generally only lived a few years. But Chopin was sick from childhood, and he lived to be nearly forty. There was no treatment for tuberculosis back then, so it is a mystery how he survived it."

"Yes," Emily adds. "And in that time, he composed hundreds of pieces of music! Right, Mr. Starek? Wasn't it two hundred and fifty or something?"

This seems an enormous number. But it fills me with joy—that means there are so many songs for me to sing!

Mr. Starek nods. "There is of course the great mystery of his talent—he composed his first piano piece at the age of seven. He was immensely gifted, and he created a kind of music that nobody had ever heard before."

"Seven?" Michael asks. He sounds impressed. "Wow...that's almost five years younger than me."

"Yes," Emily says. "It's crazy, right? Like a second grader writing a completely new piece of music. And then there's the mystery of his pianos. What I told you about, Michael. Some of them have been found and placed in museums, but there are several that are still out there in the world somewhere."

"The lost pianos," Michael says solemnly.

Mr. Starek smiles. "And don't forget the mystery of Chopin's relationship with George Sand."

"Who's he?" Michael asks.

"*She*," Emily corrects. "That was her pen name, the one she used for writing books. She was so interesting! She liked to dress as a man, to wear men's suits."

"Why did she do that?" Michael looks perplexed. "Was it a disguise?"

"No, that's just what she wore," Emily says. "And back then, men and women dressed and acted very differently from each other, so it was brave of her. The lives of women were so

restricted. She was a writer, and it was very difficult to get books published under a woman's name. She wanted to do things as easily as men did, to make a living writing books like a man, go to bars like a man, move through the world like a man. She even smoked cigars! Even though she also did a lot of things as a woman, and had many boyfriends."

"Really?" Michael is leaning forward over his knees, eyes wide. A woman dressed in suits and smoking cigars? That does sound interesting. I imagine what it would be like to put on a bright yellow suit of feathers and black cap and look like my brothers. Would I do it? To look like a boy bird? Maybe it would be fun, just for a day.

"Yes," Emily confirms. "George Sand was very independent. She has this great quote about not needing a man's help. Wait, I wrote it down." She thumbs through the pages of her notebook, smiling.

"Here. 'I ask the support of no one, neither to kill someone for me, gather a bouquet, correct a proof, nor to go with me to the theater. I go there on my own, as a man, by choice; and when I want flowers, I go on foot, by myself, to the Alps.'"

Michael looks confused. "What does she mean, kill someone for her?"

"She's just listing the kinds of things men might do for women in the 1800s," Emily says. "You know, protect them, pick flowers for them, take them to the theater. And guess what—when Chopin first met her, he couldn't tell if she was a man or a woman. But then they fell in love."

Well, this is just getting stranger and stranger.

"They did?"

Mr. Starek nods. "It was the most important relationship of his life, both personally and artistically. He did his best musical work while he was with George Sand."

"The woman who dressed like a man?" Michael asks doubtfully.

"Yes, indeed," Mr. Starek says. "They were very much in love at one point. In fact, George Sand's most famous quote is the line 'There is only one happiness in this life, to love and be loved.'"

Hmmm. That just tells me she didn't know how to SING.

"She was Chopin's muse," Emily adds. "The person who inspired him. And she had an interesting past herself. Her father was a duke or something, but her mother grew up poor. Actually, I remember reading that her grandfather ran a pool hall and sold birds on the streets—canaries and goldfinches."

Goldfinches! What do you think of that? We were popular even back then, all the way across the ocean, two hundred years ago. I bet those goldfinches had French accents.

Emily glances out the window, and I feel a warm rush, knowing she's looking for me.

Mr. Starek nods. "It wasn't an easy relationship, but Chopin's time with her was such a rich one, musically. He spent summers at her house in Nohant, in the countryside south of Paris, and he created some of his finest compositions there."

"We were just discussing that in class today!" Emily cries happily. "Chopin and George Sand were friends with a famous painter, Eugene Delacroix, who came to stay with them in Nohant. Can you imagine what that must have been like—a great musician, a great writer, and a great artist all together in one place, creating? Wait, let me find what Delacroix said about that summer. When I read it, I could picture all of them so clearly."

She sits cross-legged on the floor and turns the thin pages of her notebook again. Even from the window, I can see the small, neat lines of her handwriting on the page, like the tiny tracks of a bird. "Here. This was the summer of 1842, in Nohant. Delacroix said, 'The locality is charming and it would be difficult to find kinder hosts. When we are not together at the table or at billiards or not out on a walk, I spend time in my room or lie on the sofa. From time to time, through the open window on the garden, there enters a waft of the music of Chopin, mingled with the song of the nightingales and the scent of the roses, since he never ceases to work here.'"

I must admit, that paints a lovely picture. I can almost feel the summer breeze and smell the garden in bloom. But nightingales? *Nightingales?* Why not goldfinches? Nightingales get way too much credit in the musical department, if you ask me. Yes, all right, they can carry a tune, but they are very showy and repetitive when they sing. They don't know how to *improvise*. And isn't that the mark of musical genius? The ability to create something new?

"That was a magical year for Chopin," Mr. Starek says. "He created some extraordinary compositions. It was in the summer of 1842 that he composed the ballade in F minor. The fourth ballade."

"Which one is that?" Michael asks. "I know how to play the first ballade, the one in G minor."

"Have you not heard it?" Mr. Starek looks surprised.

"Oh, Michael," Emily says. "It's gorgeous."

Mr. Starek nods. "I find it the most beautiful of all of Chopin's compositions, and many say the most beautiful piano piece ever written. Definitely the most difficult Chopin to play."

"Is it harder than all the études and sonatas?'" Michael asks.

"In my opinion. The last ballade is very challenging from a technical standpoint, but the interpretation—the musicality of the piece—is even more so."

Michael turns to him. "Can you play it for me?"

"Oh, yes! Please!" Emily says. "I would love to hear you play it."

Mr. Starek hesitates. "I won't do it justice...but I will try."

Michael vacates the piano bench and joins Emily on the floor, where they both look at Mr. Starek with rapt attention. We are going to have a concert! I love hearing the old man play. I just hope I can restrain myself from singing along.

Mr. Starek takes out a pile of sheet music from the cupboard under the bookshelves. He searches through the pages until he finds what he's looking for, and then sets several sheets on the music rack. He sits at the piano and adjusts his hands over the keys.

The piece begins slowly, gravely. It makes me think of loneliness, of a dark bird wheeling in solitude against a gray, storm-brewing sky. Or the haunted wistfulness of Mr. Starek standing by the window in the days after his sister died. It builds plaintively, becoming faster and more desperate, and then it rushes into a river of higher notes. All of a sudden, it's not sad anymore. It's determined and exuberant, like a male goldfinch singing a mating song. Then it returns to the lonesome notes of the beginning, but this time with an overlay of fierce emotion. The music is slow and fast, sad and furious, gentle and strong.

When he finishes, Michael, Emily, and I are silent with awe.

Michael's eyes are shining. "That," he says. "That's what I want to play for the competition."

13

A Very Old Piano

Mr. Starek raises his eyebrows. "Really?"

Michael nods vigorously.

Emily and Mr. Starek exchange glances.

"Well," Mr. Starek says slowly, "it would be an excellent choice. None of the other contestants in the youth category would dare to attempt it."

"I can do it," Michael says, his face bright with certainty.

"You would need to start practicing right away. It's a tricky composition."

Michael stands up. "I want to."

"All right then," Mr. Starek says. "We can try. And good,

you've chosen your three performance pieces. Now the real work can begin."

"You can do it, Michael," Emily says. "It will be amazing."

Oh! We can do it. I know we can.

Mr. Starek smiles. "If you can master the last ballade, it will be brilliant." He pauses, his mouth twisting ruefully. "It would be even better…"

"What?" Michael waits.

Mr. Starek starts to collect the sheet music. "I was going to say, it would be even better on a Pleyel."

Michael and Emily exchange glances, and I can see that Michael wants to say something. I'm so afraid he's going to mention Halina. But instead he asks, "I still don't understand what makes that piano so special. Why was it Chopin's favorite?"

"He loved the way it sounded," Mr. Starek says. "It's hard to explain unless you can hear one for yourself. I heard a Pleyel a few years ago at a concert at the Franklin Collection, the place Emily and I were talking about. The museum allowed a visiting pianist to play Chopin on a Pleyel from the 1840s. It was just stunning. I felt as if I understood the music in an entirely different way."

"Different how?" Michael asks.

Mr. Starek considers this. "Chopin believed the Pleyel piano allowed him to hear the music inside his head. They are extraordinary instruments, a really unusual tone. It's the piano he had at Nohant, George Sand's summerhouse. The piano he used to compose Ballade number four. That's why it would be wonderful to play that piece on a Pleyel."

"I wish…" Michael's voice is wistful. He shoots Emily a quick glance, then walks to the piano, where Mr. Starek is still sitting. "Would it be okay—" he begins.

Mr. Starek seems lost in thought, and I'm not sure he's even heard Michael.

Michael swallows. "Do you think maybe we could go to your sister's house and see if she had a Pleyel? If it's still there?"

I freeze. I can feel how badly the boy wants this, because I want it, too.

The old man's forehead furrows. "Given the state of her house the last time I saw it, I'm not sure it's even safe. And as I said, I am not at all confident about the Pleyel. She had a number of upright pianos, but I never noticed a grand in her…collection."

I peer at Michael's and Emily's faces to see if they find this comment as odd as I do. How do you not notice a grand piano? It seems like it would be the main thing you *would* notice at someone's house.

Emily must be thinking the same thing because she says, "Well, she must have gotten it later, then. After you last visited. I mean, if she even had one."

Michael's shoulders drop in disappointment. "Can't we find out?"

Mr. Starek hesitates. "I do need to go to her house and take stock of things. But now that she's gone—" He stops.

"We could do that for you," Emily offers.

Her words seem to startle him, as if he is abruptly realizing where he is. I can tell he has disappeared into some memory of Halina. He looks at Emily, not understanding.

"Michael and I could," she says. "I mean, if that would help. What do you have to do at her house?"

Mr. Starek hesitates. "The people at the bank want to be paid, the money Halina owed on the house. Actually, the bank officer is coming this week. I'm not sure what he's going to propose, but it would be good to know what's in the house before I make any decisions."

Emily nods. "That makes sense. We could go over and tell you what's there."

He sighs. "Thank you, that's kind of you. But I think it is something I need to do myself."

We are all watching him. I know his face better than they do, but even Emily and Michael must be able to see the sorrow falling over it like a curtain.

"I have an idea," Emily says finally. "I could take pictures with my phone, so you can see what's in the house. Then you can go back to sort through everything when you feel ready."

Isn't that smart? Please say yes, I think.

"And we could tell you if there's a Pleyel piano!" Michael adds eagerly.

Mr. Starek looks from one to the other, still reluctant.

"Where is your sister's house?" Emily asks, already moving to the logistics.

"It's on the other side of the river, a couple of miles as the crow flies. Driving takes a bit longer because you have to cross the bridge."

Oh good. I am glad it's close—but "as the crow flies"? What makes a crow so special? We all fly the same way. Humans seem to think crows take the direct route and the rest of us birds just zigzag aimlessly around. Well, I know Mr. Starek doesn't think that. It's just an expression, but I do find it annoying.

I can tell Mr. Starek is considering the proposition. Finally, he stands up, holding the sheet music for Ballade number four and stacking it neatly.

"Actually, if you don't mind, I would appreciate that, Emily. I'll need to go eventually, but it would help me to have a sense of the state of Halina's house before my meeting with the bank officer. And to know what's there."

"Sure," Emily says. "It sounds like she had some cool stuff."

"Yes," Mr. Starek says, "but please be careful." He turns to Michael. "And I don't want you to get your hopes up about the Pleyel. Even if there is one, it wouldn't be in adequate condition to play."

"Okay," Michael says. I can tell how badly he wants for it to be there. He looks over at me, just for a second—a happy, secret look—and I hop along the branch so that he knows I'm listening.

Mr. Starek lifts his shoulders philosophically. "I guess we will find out, one way or the other."

"Wait," Michael says. "How will we know it's the Pleyel?"

Emily points to Mr. Starek's piano. "The same way we know this is an Érard. The name will be right on it."

Mr. Starek nods. "Inscribed on a small plaque," he adds. "It will likely say 'Ignace Pleyel.' He was the father of Chopin's friend Camille, and he founded the company."

"Ignace Pleyel," Michael repeats softly. "Oh, I hope it's there."

Me too! I want to hear the boy play on a piano made for the music of Chopin. And I want to sing when he does.

14

Mother's Surprise

As I fly back to the nest, I am bursting with excitement about the Pleyel piano. I just hope there really is one at Halina's house! It will be so disappointing if there isn't. Emily and Michael want to check it out as soon as possible, and when Michael called his mother, Mrs. Jin agreed to it, much to our surprise. She was so pleased that Michael had chosen his pieces for the competition that she assented quite readily, and she seemed genuinely intrigued by the idea of an antique piano.

Now there's just one problem: me. I can't have them finding that piano without me! But how do I go along? It's one thing to land on the boy's finger. But I certainly can't get in a car with them. As I'm thinking about all this, I begin to hatch a plan.

Haha, get it? That's a bird expression, "hatch a plan." And it's much better than "as the crow flies," let me tell you. You probably thought humans made it up, but birds use it, too. Like "wing it," and "fly by night," and "sitting duck." Where do you think they came from? Birds.

Actually, now that we're on the subject, here are some disrespectful things people say about birds. *Ugly duckling. For the birds. Sitting duck. Birdbrain.* Seriously? We're descended from dinosaurs, you big goofballs. Doesn't that deserve some respect? I don't think you'd call a T. rex a "birdbrain." At least not to its face.

That's okay, I forgive you. It's kind of how we birds talk about squirrels…big, clumsy brutes, the way they attack the bird feeder, spilling seeds everywhere. Why, as you know, one of them almost got Ollie killed! Even when they're not threatening our very lives, squirrels will chew right through a plastic feeder and ruin it for all of us. And they're so heavy, just the weight of a squirrel hanging on to the bird feeder can knock it straight to the ground. So no, we birds don't think much of squirrels.

But I bet squirrels feel the same way about somebody else. Maybe chipmunks.

Anyway, back to my plan. You want to know what I'm thinking? Mr. Starek said his sister's house is just across the river, so I can fly there easily if I don't try to follow Emily and Michael in the car. I mean, obviously I'm not going to fly the long way around—that would be silly! But I don't know what Halina's house looks like from above, so the tricky thing, for me, will be flying across the river and then keeping an eye out for Emily's car. I can recognize her car very easily from seeing it day after day in Mr. Starek's driveway. It's a dull gray color, like a catbird.

I'm just pondering these travel arrangements as I swoop down through the prickly holly leaves into the twiggy cavern of the tree. Mother is resting snugly in the nest. Sebastian and Oliver are nearby, squabbling over a fluff of thistledown.

"Oh good, Mirabelle, we've been waiting for you," Mother says.

I worry for a second that she's going to ask me where I've been or what I've been doing, but I can tell she has something else on her mind.

"Sebastian! Oliver!" Mother calls. "Stop that quarreling. I have something to show you."

What could it be? The boys drop the thistledown and we all line up in front of her, gripping the same branch. I wonder if she has some delicious treat to share with us. Maybe the blueberries in Mr. Starek's garden are ripe? Just the thought of them makes me hungry.

"Look," Mother says proudly. She shifts her pretty yellow breast and unfolds one wing gracefully.

There, underneath it, are three small, perfect…eggs!

They're bluish white and oval. Mother had her babies!

Sebastian, Oliver, and I are speechless, staring.

Of course we knew this day would come, but somehow it is shocking to us. If Mother has three new babies, that means Mother has babies that aren't US.

I know Sebastian and Oliver are thinking the same thing.

"Wow," Sebastian says.

"Three of them," Oliver says. "Like us."

I don't say anything.

"Yes!" Mother says. "I'm glad it isn't more. They will be easier to take care of, just three." She looks at me closely. "What do you think, Mirabelle?"

"The shells are a pretty color," I say finally.

"Aren't they? Just a hint of blue," Mother says. "And you

know what this means....In another couple of weeks, the babies will be here."

"Great," says Sebastian. He doesn't sound like he thinks it's great at all.

"So I will need more help from you three," Mother says. "And less quarreling, Sebastian and Oliver."

"Yes, Mother," we say.

"Right now, do you know how you could help? Go collect some more thistledown for the nest," she tells us. "The bottom is nicely lined, but another layer would make it beautifully soft for the new babies."

"Yes, Mother," we say.

We fly out of the holly tree and over Mr. Starek's fence. There, below us, is the grassy meadow where the thistles grow. The sun is shining warmly, and the purple heads of the thistles bob luxuriously in the light breeze.

My brothers each land on a thistle, gripping the stalk. I land just below a spiky bloom and start plucking the soft down.

"We're being replaced," Sebastian announces glumly.

"Yeah," Oliver says. "Three eggs, one for each of us."

"Thtop," I say, spitting out thistle. I am not feeling good about it, either, but my role with my brothers is always to calm things down. "You knew she was going to lay eggs. That's why she's been working so hard on the nest."

"I just didn't think it would be this soon," Oliver protests.

"She won't have time for us after the new babies come," Sebastian says. "We'll be the old babies, which means we might as well be grown-up."

That is a terrible thought. We don't want to be grown-up.

"Well, there's nothing we can do about it," I say. "Those babies are coming whether we like it or not."

"Yeah." Oliver sighs.

"I don't see why we have to make things so comfortable for them," Sebastian complains. "They're not *our* babies."

"It's not for them, it's for Mother," I correct him.

Oliver brightens. "Yeah, if we help Mother, maybe she won't forget about us."

"She's not going to forget about us! She's our MOTHER," I protest. "The new babies won't change that."

But inside, I am not so sure. New babies take a lot of time and attention. And they are so little and delicate. In the past week, eggs have started hatching in hidden nests all over the backyard, and our aunts and uncles and cousins have been very busy. Soon that will be Mother.

"On the bright side," Sebastian offers, "she will have less time to pay attention to what *we're* doing. Ollie, maybe we can start going to the Garcias' feeder on our own."

The Garcias, next door to Mr. Starek, have a giant bird feeder mounted on a pole in the middle of their backyard. It is a vertical tube with interesting little wooden perches and holes you poke your beak through to gobble seeds. Sebastian and Oliver love it, but Mother will only let us feed there when she can go with us. It is such a large and elaborate bird feeder that it attracts all kinds of much bigger birds, and it's out in the open in the Garcias' back-yard, so she's afraid a hawk might spot us, or one of the redheaded woodpeckers or blue jays.

You didn't think a bird would eat another bird, did you? Well, I am ashamed to say so, but it happens. It's called cannibalism, same as in humans.

See? We have a lot in common.

"Mother will know if you try to do that," I warn them. "And you could get eaten!"

"Well, she might not even care, now that she has three new babies to replace us," Oliver says mournfully.

We are all so dejected at this thought that we can barely summon the energy to pick the thistledown. But we do it anyway, plucking soft, generous beak-fuls from the waving heads of the thistles.

At least with our mouths overflowing with fluff, we can no longer talk about all the ways life is going to change when Mother has three new babies. We fly back to the nest.

Mother rises eagerly when she sees us. She takes the thistle-down and starts smoothing it around, tucking it gently under the eggs.

"Did you have trouble?" she asks, concerned. "That took lon-ger than I expected."

"No," I tell her. "We were just taking our time. It's such a nice day."

"Is it?" Mother asks. "I can hardly tell in here, and I won't be able to leave the nest for a while now." She admires the soft new layer of fluff. "Oh, this is lovely! Thank you, thank you. I knew I could count on you three."

That makes us feel better.

Mother continues fussing over the nest. "I have an idea. Would you like to think of names for the babies?"

What?! We get to name the babies?

"Really?" Oliver asks. "Anything we want?"

"Well, I want their names to be beautiful, like your names. But yes, you can help me think of good ones."

"But we don't know if they're girls or boys," Sebastian says.

"True, but you can come up with your three favorite girls' names and your three favorite boys' names, and then when the eggs hatch, we'll choose."

"Mirabelle can think of the girl names," Sebastian says. "Ollie and I will do the boys."

"I might have ideas for boy names, too," I say, irritated. Why should Sebastian get to decide?

"We need six names, so there are plenty of chances for you all to think of ones you like," Mother reproaches us gently.

"What about Annabelle?" I ask. I am thinking it would be nice if one of the babies had a name that sounds a bit like mine.

Mother smiles. "That's nice."

"What about Mortimer?" Oliver suggests.

Sebastian nearly falls off his branch laughing. "Mortimer! That's a terrible idea. That bird sounds boring before he's even born."

"I like it," Oliver says stubbornly.

"Then it is on our list," Mother says. "And Sebastian, why don't you come up with ideas of your own, instead of making fun of Oliver's?"

So that is how the day ends, with all of us talking about names for the babies. It is a little scary that there will be new babies, but a little exciting, too. And we get to name them!

And even though I didn't say so at the time, I am thinking that Sebastian is probably right that Mother will soon be way too busy to keep a close eye on us. Maybe, just maybe, that will give me more time for my adventures with Michael and Emily, and our search for the lost piano.

15

The House Full of Treasures

Two days later, I wait in the big maple tree in Mr. Starek's front yard, hidden in a crowd of leaves, watching for Emily's gray car. This time, she leaves Michael in the car and runs up to the front door by herself. I flutter over to the bell so she'll see me.

"Mirabelle!" Emily cries. "I was hoping you'd be here."

Mr. Starek comes outside to talk to her, and they stand on the stoop gazing over the summery yard, where everything is thick and green and blooming.

"Here is the key to the house," he says. "And I gave you the address. Call me if you have any trouble." He waves to Michael.

"Sure," says Emily. She lowers her voice. "Michael made good choices for the competition, don't you think? The prelude and the étude will both show off his finger work. But the fourth ballade…do you think he can learn to play that in a month?"

"It is a very challenging piece," Mr. Starek allows. "Some of the best pianists do not play it well. But it's not so much the time as the talent that matters. Michael—well, if he can do it, he has a good shot at winning. There's a magic in the way he plays Chopin. Such intensity, such grace."

"I know!" Emily says. "It's like this music has been waiting for him his whole life."

I can't help but feel they are talking about me when they say these things, and my heart swells with pride. I am singing when Michael plays, and it *is* magic. Nothing has ever sounded the way we sound together. I want them to go on and on—tell me specifics!—but Michael is waiting in the car, impatient, and it's time for our trip to Halina's house.

Well, I say "our," but of course they don't know I'm coming. I fly up, up, up to the very top branches of the big maple so I can watch Emily's sedan proceed down Mr. Starek's street. Then I soar up into the clear sky, until I'm looking down on the dark rooftops and the patchwork of green lawns. In one, I see a glistening swimming pool, like a bright drop of blue paint. Children are racing around it, jumping in with impressive splashes, and from this height, their swimsuits are little sprinkles of color.

We goldfinches are tiny birds, but when I get up this high, it's the human world that looks tiny, so small that I could fit Mr.

Starek's house under my wing. Emily's car is like a shiny gray pebble rolling along. When she turns to cross the steel bridge, I keep an eye on it, flying across the broad, swirling river and into a new neighborhood.

Sebastian, Oliver, and I have done this a few times, and Mother gives permission as long as we only land in the high tops of trees. She doesn't want us actually going down into people's yards, because you never know what might be waiting there. Not just cats or hawks or bird feeders dangerously out in the open, but sometimes an awful kid with a BB gun. We are terrified of BB guns.

I fly from tree to tree on the other side of the river, looking down at strange roofs and unfamiliar backyards. The houses are different over here, smaller and farther apart, with tangled woods in between.

I am just starting to worry that I won't see Emily and Michael, and won't be able to find Halina's house, when I spot the gray car. It is going slowly on the road, and finally turns into the driveway of a two-story house with a sagging roof. The house is a dingy white, and everything about it looks ramshackle and untended. The yard is thick with tall weeds, the front porch is tilted and splintering, and the walkway is chipped and hidden by grass. But the house has tall windows with lots of panes, and I can tell that at one point, it was nice, maybe even fancy.

Michael hops out of the car and stands in the middle of the weed-filled yard. "Wow," he says. "This place looks bad."

Emily frowns. "Yeah. It's so different from Mr. Starek's."

I fly down to the broken railing of the porch to have a closer look, and Michael shouts, "Hey! It's Mirabelle."

Emily laughs. "It's just another goldfinch," she says. "They're all over this time of year."

What?!

I am very disappointed in Emily. I hop along the railing and cock my head at them.

"No, it's her," Michael says. "I can tell."

Good boy.

He raises his hand and stretches it toward me. "Mirabelle," he calls.

Oh, here we go again.

But I need for them to know it's *me*. I fly to him and land on his finger, just for an instant, looking up at him. Then I flutter away.

Emily gasps. "It *is* Mirabelle!" she says. "She must have followed us here! That's incredible."

Yes. Thank you.

Michael laughs. "See? She wants to find the piano, too!"

"Well, let's have a look inside," Emily says.

Now, should I go inside this strange house? I cringe thinking of what Mother would say. But I want so badly to see whether there's a Pleyel piano here! And I won't be able to tell what's going on if I wait out in the yard.

So when Emily turns the key in the lock and pushes the door open, I hesitate only for a second. Even though it's dark inside, and it smells musty and stale, and specks of dust float in the thin beams of sunlight, as soon as Emily and Michael step through the doorway, I fly after them.

I land on the top of the door so it will be easy for me to escape, and boy oh boy, am I glad I did.

The inside of the house is like a gloomy, dense forest, with no way out. I have never seen so much *stuff* in my entire life. The dark living room is filled to the brim with furniture, paintings, trunks, china. There are stacks of old books on the floor, piles of chipped crockery. I see a box filled with dusty glass figurines. There are three sets of fireplace andirons—only one of which is by the fireplace—and a dozen floor lamps, with intricate floral-patterned brass stands, colorful tasseled shades.

And musical instruments! Oh my goodness. I almost don't see them at first, in the darkness, in the density of things. But as I scan the room, I notice two cellos leaning against a wall where the wallpaper is sloughing off in long, shabby strips. A harp stands upright in one corner. And pianos...oh yes, pianos. Four upright pianos, scratched and dusty, are crowded together in the center of the room, pressed against one another in a way that would make them impossible to play.

"Whoa," Michael says.

He and Emily can barely step beyond the front door. I don't think they've even noticed that I flew inside.

"There's so much stuff." He looks around in amazement.

It's true. Every surface of every couch, chair, and table is piled high with books or dishes or knickknacks, shoeboxes overflowing with knots of jewelry, plastic containers of linens, yellow with age.

Emily gazes around the room, stunned. "Mr. Starek said his sister was a collector. This isn't collecting. It's hoarding."

Michael looks puzzled. "What's that? Why are there so many books...and dishes?"

Emily hesitates. "Well, it's what he said, a kind of mental illness. She couldn't help herself, I guess."

Poor Halina. No wonder Mr. Starek barely saw her. There was no room for even one more person in this house.

"Look!" Michael cries. "FOUR pianos." He points.

"Yes," Emily says, "I see them, but they're all uprights."

Yes, all straight-backed, tall pianos, like the one at Mr. Starek's house.

Michael clambers over a sofa to have a closer look. "But four of them! She must have been RICH."

Emily shakes her head. "You remember what Mr. Starek said. They aren't worth anything."

"Well, I would like to have four pianos," Michael says.

"Why?" Emily asks. "You only need one to play."

I think of how Oliver, when he was a baby, liked to collect things and bring them back to the nest: bits of string, a button, a shiny scrap of foil. Mother had to convince him that you could admire things and appreciate them without *having* them, that birds don't need to keep anything they can't eat or use. Halina clearly didn't feel that way.

Emily picks her way across the obstacle course of the room, through the teetering piles of books, stepping over boxes of trinkets, turning on a lamp. The arc of yellow lamplight only shows how dirty the place is, how tightly packed with things.

Emily sneezes. "I think we should open some windows. It smells moldy in here."

Michael climbs over a footstool and an end table to unlatch a window. He tries to open it. "It's stuck," he reports.

"Try another one," Emily tells him.

When she reaches the pianos, she shakes her head. "None of them are Pleyels."

I stay where I am, clutching the top of the door. Is that it? Aren't we going to check out the rest of the place?

"It could be in another room," Michael says.

"Yeah," Emily agrees. "But how are we going to get to it? Look, the stairs are blocked."

There are more cardboard boxes on the stairs, more stacks of books.

"I guess I should take some pictures," Emily says doubtfully.

Michael nods. "You told Mr. Starek you would."

"I don't know how he'll be able to tell a thing about what's in the house." Emily scans the crowded space. "It's all so crammed together."

She turns on a few more lights and takes out her phone, carefully snapping pictures, moving slowly in a circle.

"Honestly," she says, "if the people from the bank are willing to deal with all this, Mr. Starek should let them. It's a mess. I don't see how he could ever sort through it himself."

"But what about the Pleyel?" Michael protests. "The grand piano? We have to look for it."

Emily is still taking pictures. "How are we going to check out the other rooms? It's like everything is barricaded off."

"A grand piano is pretty big," Michael says. "We'll see it."

Emily looks dubious. "We can try, but I really don't think we should go upstairs. I mean, if there's as much stuff up there as there is down here, I'd be worried about the whole house collapsing."

"Yikes," Michael says, glancing up at the ceiling.

Now I'm worried, too. But it's a lot easier for me to look around than it is for them. I'm little, and I can *fly*. The heaps of furniture aren't going to stop me.

I flutter from the doorway to the other side of the living room, landing on a dusty green lampshade.

"Look!" Michael cries. "Mirabelle is in here."

"Oh dear," Emily says. "I hope we can get her out. Push the door open wider."

"Mirabelle," Michael calls. "This way."

I ignore him and fly over a tangle of wooden chairs into another dark, crowded room. This one has a big table in the center of it and a fancy chandelier hanging from the ceiling. It must be the dining room, and it's as jam-packed as the living room. I peer through the dusty gloom at the broad table heaped with china and glassware. No pianos in here.

"Mirabelle, that's the wrong way," Emily is calling, but I've already flown out of the dining room into what seems to be the kitchen. It's hard to tell because all the usual appurtenances— oven, sink, counters—are covered with stacks of books, photographs, and boxes of figurines.

There's definitely not a piano in here.

The last room, through the doorway of the kitchen, seems to

be a kind of study. It's dark—there's a large window, but a heavy curtain is blocking it. This room is every bit as crowded as the rest of the house. I flutter to the top of a wingback chair to look around. My eyes have to get used to the gloom. In front of me is a massive wooden table stacked with plates and painted vases. Pressed next to it are several dark chairs with pretty floral carvings across the backs. Two battered, black instrument cases lean against each other in one corner, surrounded by more cardboard boxes, their contents overflowing.

I fly over to the table to have a closer look. When I land on the porcelain rim of one of the vases, I can see that the table is made of beautiful wood, despite the darkness and the dust. It is reddish brown and full of swirls. And then I see something else.

Over the edge of the table, in the shadows, is a geometric pattern of black and white that I would recognize anywhere. The keys of a piano.

16

A Grand Piano

It's not a table at all! It's a piano, a grand piano! I hop down to one of the black keys, feeling its cool, smooth surface beneath my feet. There are curly gold letters on the face of the piano, but how am I to know what they say? I need Emily and Michael. Now!

I jump up and down on the black key, landing as hard as I can. Even so, it barely makes a sound. We goldfinches are too small to really throw our weight around. But the key *does* produce a thin, high note, again and again as my feet strike it.

I can hear Emily and Michael talking in the other room. After a few seconds of me hopping and hopping, they stop.

Michael says, "What's that?"

I keep hopping forcefully on the piano key, listening to its faint *plink, plink, plink.*

A minute later, they are standing in the doorway of the study.

"Oh—look at Mirabelle!" Michael sucks in his breath.

Emily gasps. "It's a grand piano." She crawls over furniture and squirms between boxes to get to me.

"Michael, pull open that curtain," Emily says, and Michael scrambles to tug the dark, heavy curtain across the window. It rattles over the rod, and abruptly, sunlight pours through the dusty panes. We can finally see what's here.

Emily stretches her T-shirt and gently wipes dust from the broad top. The piano is huge, and as I flutter around it, I see the gleaming waves and curls in the wood, so unusual a pattern they might be a painting. On the side are two brass ornaments, flowerlike, and at each end of the keyboard is a carved scroll almost in the shape of a sideways treble clef. The whole piano is a work of art.

Emily bends over the piano keys, her face so close to mine that I am looking straight into her sparkling brown eyes.

But she isn't looking at me. She rubs her palm over a gold-colored rectangular plaque inlaid in the face of the piano, above the keys.

"Michael," she breathes, her voice barely more than a whisper.

She touches one slim finger to the plaque and reads reverently, "'Ignace Pleyel.'"

I think I am going to faint.

Michael is beside her now, eyes wide. "We did it!" he shouts. "We did it! We found the Pleyel!" They hug each other ecstatically.

Now wait, what's this "we" business? Have they forgotten who really found the piano? Oh, but who cares! It's the Pleyel piano! The kind that Chopin *himself* played two hundred years ago!

I fly up to perch on a lampshade. I'll have a better view from here.

"Let's move all this stuff off it so I can take a picture for Mr. Starek," Emily says.

A thick layer of dust shrouds the surface Emily didn't wipe, but as Michael begins to lift things off the top of the piano, I can see patches of clean wood underneath. It's not the dark wood of the piano at Mr. Starek's house. This piano is a rich red-brown color, and there are swirling, dappled patterns that catch the light, like water in a stream.

"Look how beautiful it is," Emily whispers. "It's not like any piano I've ever seen."

"Me neither," Michael agrees. "Can I play it?" His fingers reach for the keys, but Emily grabs his arm.

"No, don't," she says. "Not yet. It won't sound right with all these things on it, and I'm sure it needs to be tuned."

Michael looks disappointed, but I know what she means. Somehow, if the piano doesn't sound perfect, the spell will be broken.

With the top cleared off and the furniture and boxes that immediately surround the piano pushed aside, Emily holds up her phone and begins taking pictures. She moves away from the piano, carefully photographing the full length of it.

A second later, her phone rings.

"Hi, Mr. Starek," she says, laughing. "Yes! Can you believe it? It's a Pleyel."

She listens for a minute and then says, "Okay, that's what we'll do. Yes. Yes, I know! It's incredible."

When she hangs up, she turns to Michael. "Let's finish taking pictures of the other rooms for him. He says we should try to clear out this room a bit so he can have his piano tuner take a look at it."

So that is how we spend the day. Emily and Michael work much harder than I do, naturally. They are lifting and sorting, moving boxes out of the study and scooting furniture to the sides of the room. They clear the piles off the stairs.

I mostly spend the morning exploring the rest of the house. I have never been inside a human house before! Of course, I know what they look like from peeking into so many windows. But Mr. Starek's house is clean and tidy, as orderly as his freshly mown lawn, with its crisp green edges. It's not at all like this. Halina's house is like the wild brambles of the meadow—dark and tangled and almost impenetrable. How did someone live here? I never met Halina, but now I am beginning to know her, through the thicket of her things.

There are many musical instruments. All the upright pianos, and this grand piano, long and magnificent. Three or four cellos in cases, and a few violins. When I fly upstairs, through the labyrinth of dark, crowded bedrooms, I find another harp, standing elegantly in a corner. Did Halina play the harp? I swoop over to it and grip one of its strings, hanging sideways and surveying the cluttered landscape—boxes and boxes of forgotten things, dusty piles of books, stacked china plates, jumbles of glassware, and several huge, dark paintings leaning against the walls.

Where did Halina get all this stuff? And what is Mr. Starek going to do with it, now that she's gone?

When we finally leave the house, Michael holds the door wide for me. I soar out into the daylight, the rush of clean air filling my lungs. He takes a deep breath, too, and smiles up at me. It is good to be out in the light, out in the open again.

It is late afternoon by the time we get back to Mr. Starek's house—I get there first, with my aerial shortcut—and I see immediately that there's a visitor. A car I don't recognize is in the driveway.

When Emily's car pulls in, Mr. Starek opens the front door and comes out onto the porch with a thin, gray sort of man. He reminds me of a tufted titmouse—drab-looking but with something official and alert about him.

"And as I was saying, we will take care of everything for you," the strange man says. "I know this is a difficult time."

"Yes." Mr. Starek nods. "It is. I would greatly appreciate it if the bank could delay taking action for a few more weeks. I haven't even had a chance to go through my sister's belongings."

The man makes a sympathetic clucking noise and lifts his briefcase. "I'll do my best, but it's really up to the chief mortgage officer. Your sister was carrying significant debt. The bank will likely decide to move ahead with a sale."

Emily and Michael come up the walkway, looking curious. "Sale of what?" Emily asks.

"Ah, here you are," Mr. Starek says. "Emily, Michael, this is Mr. Popinski from the bank. He is going to help me dispose of Halina's estate."

Estate? That sounds like a fancy word for the shabby house crammed with stuff.

Mr. Starek turns back to the gray man. "The house is in no state to be put on the market right now."

The man dismisses this comment with a wave of his hand. "Oh, believe me, I'm sure we've seen worse. You should think of the bank—all of us at the bank—as a resource for you in this unfortunate situation. We're here to help."

"I appreciate that," Mr. Starek says, "but the biggest help you could give me is a little more time."

Mr. Popinski nods briskly. "As I said, I will try to accommodate you. But if that's not possible, we'll take care of selling the house and contents and use the proceeds to settle your sister's debts."

What?! House *and* contents? Does that mean the Pleyel?

"Thank you for coming here personally," Mr. Starek says. "I know I should have been in touch with you sooner."

"That's quite all right, Mr. Starek," Mr. Popinski says. "We'll sort this out promptly, and let you get back to your life."

He lifts a hand in farewell and proceeds down the walkway to his car.

Emily and Michael are as alarmed as I am.

"Sell Halina's house?" Michael says, turning to Mr. Starek. "But you can't! We just found the piano."

"You did," Mr. Starek tells him, "and I can't wait to see it. But I'm afraid we may not have much time. Halina had taken out a large loan that she hadn't paid back, and it's within the bank's rights to take possession of the house."

Emily's smooth forehead creases with worry. "Just the house?" she asks. "Or everything inside, too?"

"Let's cross that bridge when we come to it," Mr. Starek says. "Right now there's a Pleyel piano that we need to get into shape. I can't believe she actually had one! She was telling the truth this whole time."

17

Pieces of a Picture

We have so much to do! Mr. Starek calls his regular piano tuner, who goes to Halina's house to assess the condition of the Pleyel. Amazingly, it is not in as terrible shape as everyone feared. In fact, the tuner tells Mr. Starek that its owners must have taken good care of it over the years, at least until the last decade. The tuner says it is a very old piano—we don't know how old exactly, but Emily is determined to find out—but it was carefully restored a while ago, and he has to make only minor adjustments to get it ready to play. Someone maintained the piano very well.

"That must have been before Halina found it at the estate sale," Mr. Starek says. "But clearly she could tell it was something special." He shakes his head in wonder. "I am learning new things about Halinka even now, after she's gone."

Halinka is his pet name for her, and I've only heard him say it once. I don't think the old man has thought of her as Halinka in a long time.

While the Pleyel is being tuned, the lessons continue at Mr. Starek's house, and Michael is making great progress. I can hear him getting more fluid and confident in the notes, and even my own voice gets stronger and more sure every time we warm up together.

Still, the fourth ballade is a very difficult piece. The transitions between the movements are particularly hard for the boy.

"I don't understand why Chopin wrote it this way," Michael complains in frustration.

"The key," Mr. Starek tells him, "is to keep the simple parts simple, so the complexity of the piece builds and astonishes at the end."

Michael grunts, but I can't tell whether it's in agreement or resistance.

One day, as the lesson is wrapping up and Mr. Starek is putting away sheet music and Emily is packing up her things, Michael says, "I want to see what he looks like."

At first, I don't know who Michael is talking about, but Mr. Starek understands immediately. "Chopin? There are very few images of him."

"And the lady, too, the one with the boy's name."

"George Sand," Emily chimes in. "Here, I can pull up pictures on my laptop."

Ooooh, I want to see what they look like, too! We've been talking and talking about them. I want to put faces to these names.

Emily opens her computer and her fingers tap the keyboard. "Let's see…I'm only finding one photograph. Does that seem right?"

"Is it the daguerreotype? By Bisson?" Mr. Starek asks. "I have a copy of it on the wall somewhere." He glances around the room, and we look at all the serious faces of the great composers, staring back at us.

"That one," Emily says, pointing. I cannot see at all with their big heads in the way. I take a chance and hop down to the windowsill, peering through the screen at an angle.

Hanging low on the wall is a black-and-white picture of

a pale, dark-haired, worried-looking fellow. He is dressed in a fussy, old-fashioned suit, and his hands are crossed on his lap.

Are those the hands that made such beautiful music? The fingers are thin and elegant— I can see that. But his gaze is pained, as if it hurts him just to sit there.

"He looks different than I expected," Michael says. "He doesn't look very happy."

"Yeah," Emily agrees. "He seems kind of miserable. This one is much better." She lifts the computer and turns it toward Mr. Starek, who smiles in recognition.

"That's the painting by Delacroix," he says. "The painter whose words you read to us, about the summers he spent at George Sand's estate with Chopin."

This picture is so vibrant I startle—vivid with colors, white and gold, deep oranges and browns, crisp shades of black. It's a close portrait of a man's face. He has an intense expression, and his hair is the soft russet of a female cardinal, falling back from his face in luxuriant waves.

Mr. Starek continues, "This is a fragment of a much bigger painting—actually, the full canvas was a picture of Chopin sitting at his piano, playing for George Sand."

"Oh, right," Emily says. "I've seen that picture of her. Look, Michael, here's the other piece." She types for a few seconds, then turns the laptop toward Michael.

I see a woman painted in the same vivid style as the Chopin portrait, her dark head tilted to the side, her creamy arms crossed over her lap. Her eyes are downcast, as if she's overcome with feeling.

"Notice her expression," Mr. Starek says. "The original canvas showed Chopin sitting at the piano and George Sand sitting

131

behind him, reacting to the music as he played. She looks very emotional here. Delacroix prized this painting. He kept it in his studio until he died."

Emily nods. "Because it was of his friends."

"But why would somebody cut it into pieces?" Michael demands.

"I suppose they thought they could make more money selling it as two portraits," Mr. Starek says. "A portrait of Chopin and one of George Sand. Both pictures are hanging in European museums now. And those are only two parts of the original canvas—it was very large, and the remaining piece showed the living room and the piano as well."

"I wish we could look at the whole thing," Michael says. "You can't even see his hands at the piano. Just his head. He could be doing anything."

Mr. Starek nods. "Yes, it's a shame. But this gives you a better sense of Chopin than the photograph. It shows his passion for music, for life."

Emily pulls up the two portraits side by side on the screen and tilts her head, considering them. "You can tell they were being painted by a friend, don't you think?"

She's right about that. Not only do the faces of Chopin and George Sand have such vivid expressions, but you get the sense that whoever was painting them had great affection for them, and that warmth of feeling flowed through his brush. He wanted to capture their *personalities*, not just the way they looked.

Just like I know Halina a little from her house and her piano, I feel like I know these two a little from these fragments of a painting. And seeing the flood of emotions in their faces makes me all the more excited to hear the sound of Halina's Pleyel.

18

To Play a Pleyel

While I can hardly wait for the day of the first lesson on the Pleyel, I must admit, I'm a little worried about how things will go over at Halina's house. Will Michael get to warm up alone? Can he and I still perform our duets? I certainly hope so, but in the new setting, I'm not so sure.

Which is all to say, I'm both nervous and excited on the day that Mr. Starek arranges for Michael to have his first lesson at Halina's. Truth be told, Mr. Starek probably feels the same way. I know that he has visited the house several times now, with the piano tuner and with Emily. I'm sure the first time was hard for him...to go to Halina's house and be surrounded by her things, with Halina herself gone. But I think, with the discovery of the piano, it's almost as if he's getting his sister back, bit by bit.

Today, he has asked Mrs. Jin to bring Michael to the lesson, instead of Emily. Perhaps he wants to talk to her about the festival, which is now only three weeks away! I've hidden myself in the rosebush by Halina's sagging porch, where I have a good view of the front door. When Mrs. Jin steps out of her car, I can see immediately that she has reservations about this new locale for Michael's lessons. She stands in the overgrown yard, head angled to one side, lips pursed, staring at the dilapidated house.

Michael comes charging over the weedy path, his face bright and full of excitement.

"Welcome!" Mr. Starek calls from the porch.

Seeing Mrs. Jin's expression, he beckons Michael into the house and then steps down into the yard. "I know it's not much to look at. The house has fallen into disrepair. But the important thing is, my sister's Pleyel is in excellent condition. I am very eager to have Michael play it. I think the instrument itself can prepare him for the competition better than I can."

Mrs. Jin picks her way across the rough path. "He is thrilled about getting a chance to play it," she says. "I heard him on the phone with his father—he couldn't stop talking about it. He could hardly sleep last night." She pauses. "It's just remarkable that your sister had such an old and unusual piano, without you even knowing it."

"It is, it is," Mr. Starek agrees.

Mrs. Jin stands at the bottom of the porch steps, surveying the shabby house. To me, it has become a magical place that has a Pleyel—a real Pleyel—but I can only imagine how it looks to her. "May I just ask, Michael won't be playing this kind of piano in the competition, right? You said it would likely be a Steinway?"

"Yes," Mr. Starek says.

"Then I'm not sure I understand—what's the value of practicing on this antique piano? It's so different from what he'll have to play when he competes."

Mr. Starek takes a moment before answering. "I know it may sound odd," he says finally. "But the difference between the young contestants at the Chopin Festival is less likely to be technical expertise—they'll all be impressive—than an artistic quality, a musicality that shows their depth of understanding and affinity for Chopin. It's not something I can easily teach Michael. But if he plays Chopin's music on the very type of piano Chopin composed on...well, I think he will acquire that artistry almost by..." Mr. Starek struggles for the right word. "Osmosis."

Mother has taught us about osmosis—it's how the plants in Mr. Starek's garden soak up water. Is that what he means? He wants Michael to soak up Chopin the way a thirsty plant absorbs water?

"Just by playing a Pleyel?" Mrs. Jin asks. She looks skeptical, but I know she trusts the old man.

"I do think so, yes," Mr. Starek says. "I've heard top pianists comment that after playing Chopin on a Pleyel, they were able

136

to bring a new intuition and imaginative freedom to their performances on other kinds of pianos. It is worth a try, at least. If Michael doesn't make the progress I'm hoping for, we can always revert to my piano at home for the final lessons."

Mrs. Jin's eyes flit over the silhouette of the house, and I can tell she's taking it all in, the sagging roof, the peeling paint, the grime. "Of course I'll defer to your judgment," she says. "Emily is going to pick Michael up for me, so perhaps we can talk by phone after the lesson."

"Certainly. Would you like to see the piano?"

She smiles. "Oh yes. Michael says I have to see it."

As Mr. Starek leads her into the house, I fly around the side to the window of the study. There's an overgrown rhododendron near it, so I land on its dark leaves and peer through the dusty windowpane.

Michael is sitting on the piano bench. He glances up when I reach the bush and grins. He's been watching for me.

The first thing I notice is that Emily and Mr. Starek have done an excellent job of clearing the clutter from the study. The piano is now in the middle of the room, with a wide berth around it. The other items—the instruments, the chairs, the vases—have been removed, or carefully pushed to the side.

They have also tidied things up. The surfaces of the bookshelves and lamps, and most of all, the Pleyel, are no longer thick with dust but sleek and shining.

The piano itself is—well, there's no other word for it but *magnificent*. I can't stop staring at its gleaming red-brown surface and the swirling, watery patterns in the wood. They are so distinctive, like a portrait of a river: dark splotches and light ripples, a shape like a wave, a shape like a lily pad. The piano's lid is raised, and I glimpse the complicated array of strings and hammers inside.

Mr. Starek and Mrs. Jin stand in the doorway.

"Oh, Michael," Mrs. Jin says. "I can see why you were so excited about this. What a lovely, lovely instrument." She walks toward it, and when her eyes shine with wonder, it is easy to see Michael in her, and even to see the young girl she once was, who also played the piano.

Maybe there is something magic about this piano, I think. It cracks people open like I crack open the husks of sunflower seeds, and what you see then is their soft, essential core.

She strokes the side of the Pleyel with one finger. "Can I hear you play it?"

Oh dear. I am suddenly nervous about what will happen next. What if Mr. Starek and Mrs. Jin want Michael to start playing right now? Or what if Michael himself is so enraptured with this new piano that he charges ahead without remembering me? Will he play this beautiful piano for the first time without me?

My heart is beating so hard I can barely think.

But then Michael asks, "Sure, but can I have a few minutes to warm up?"

I feel a rush of relief. He remembered!

"Of course," Mr. Starek says, turning to Mrs. Jin. "It's his routine. It gets him in the right frame of mind to do his best work."

"Oh yes, I understand," Mrs. Jin says, though her voice is tinged with wistfulness. "Well, I don't want to interfere. I will hear it another time. Have a good lesson, Michael. Emily will come for you in an hour or so."

"Are you sure you don't want to wait?"

Michael's mother shakes her head. "You have important work to do," she says, "and I don't want to disrupt Michael's lesson."

"Let me walk you to your car," Mr. Starek says, and when they leave the study, Michael and I are finally alone.

I hop excitedly up and down on my branch.

I can't wait to hear what this Pleyel sounds like...or what I sound like with this Pleyel!

Michael turns toward me. "Watch out, Mirabelle. I'm going to open the window so I can hear you better."

I retreat into the dense leaf cover while he pushes on the window. It sticks, so he bangs it with the palm of his hand. Finally, he opens it a few inches, and the musty smell of the room envelops me. I ruffle my feathers in distaste, but I come closer to the window, ready to sing.

Michael leans forward, his back straight, his fingers curled over the keys. He begins to play the Minute Waltz, our old favorite.

But it sounds *different*. I nearly fall off the branch. I am so startled, I forget to sing.

This piano sounds both clearer and softer somehow. The music has a lushness, a gentle fullness that is nothing like Mr. Starek's Érard. The high notes are silvery. The middle ones are velvety and rich. The low notes ring out sonorous and strong. Michael looks over at me in amazement and laughs with joy.

We have never heard anything like this before. The notes, frilly and delicate, mingle and linger in the air. I realize a piano can have a voice, just like a bird has a voice and a human has a voice. And the voice of the Pleyel is so delicate and clear, it gilds the air. Everything around me shimmers. Oh, it is glorious!

Now *my* voice finds the melody and I burst into song.

Michael's face splits with a wide smile. He plays faster, his fingers dancing over the keys. I sing and sing, barely able to catch my breath. It's like we are racing each other, but when we get to the finish line—the end of the waltz—we cross it together, as one.

When the last note rings through the quiet room, Michael sits back, staring at the piano.

He looks over at me. "Now I know why this was his favorite. It sounds *amazing*."

We sit there in silence for a minute, contemplating the wonder of the Pleyel.

"Let's try the one we were practicing," Michael says finally.

Oh, he means the tricky étude! We're getting good at it, but we definitely need to practice. How will it sound on the Pleyel?

I listen to him play the slow opening bars, holding my breath at their graceful, somber tones. And then comes the thrilling rush of notes, and I open my beak and *sing*.

The strange, forlorn, fierce music of a winter wind fills the room, spilling through the open window to where I'm sitting. Even though the day is hot and the shade is warm and humid, I can feel the chill in the music...the slicing, unrelenting force of some distant wind roaring.

Michael's fingers leap and dance over the keys, so fast they barely seem to touch the surfaces. My breast swells and the music soars through me.

When the last note fades into silence, Michael and I look at each other. Something is happening to us. The music is flowing through us the way a river flows to the sea. It doesn't matter that he's a boy and I'm a bird; what we are right now is just a way for the music to go where it needs to go, streaming out into the air.

There's a soft knock on the study door, and I retreat into the cluster of rhododendron leaves.

Mr. Starek and Emily enter together. I've been so caught up in my singing that I didn't even realize Emily had arrived. My heart leaps a little every time I see her, with her crest of brown locks and her quick, curious movements. Emily really would make a fine bird.

Mr. Starek is shaking his head in amazement. "Truly astonishing, Michael. I can't believe how well you're doing, all on your own."

"You've had a breakthrough!" Emily exclaims. "I knew you would."

Michael's cheeks turn pink, and he looks down at the piano keys.

Would this breakthrough have happened without the Pleyel? And without me keeping Michael company? I doubt it, but it's easy for me not to care. It is good for Michael to get the credit and the boost of confidence. I know that confidence is a big part of being able to play well, or to sing well, for that matter. It takes not just skill to excel, but faith. You have to feel certain you can do it.

"Can you see now what I was talking about? The way Chopin's music was made for a Pleyel?" Mr. Starek asks.

Michael nods reverently, his eyes fixed on the piano.

Emily touches the keyboard. "It's both more delicate and more...ornate, somehow."

"The notes go on and on," Mr. Starek says. "Even without the pedal. This is what Chopin intended for you to hear."

We are quiet then, and I know we are all thinking of Chopin sitting at a Pleyel piano nearly two centuries ago, composing his preludes and études and ballades.

Emily runs her finger lightly over the keys. "Wouldn't it be cool to know how old this piano is?" she says. "I'm going to ask my professor how to figure out its age."

Mr. Starek sighs. "I wish Halina were still here to tell us about it."

He pulls a chair close to the piano bench and sits down. "I have some pointers for you, Michael, but I want you to pay attention to your own instincts."

Michael nods eagerly and leans forward again, ready to play. I settle on my perch to watch the rest of the lesson.

It isn't long now until the competition. Will Michael be ready in time? Will he be good enough to win?

19

Practice

Day after day, this is what we do. Well, the lessons aren't actually every day—but they've gone from three or four times a week to almost daily, in preparation for the competition. And you know what's funny? When Michael practices the same piece over and over again, I never get bored. It doesn't feel like he's repeating something in endless succession. It feels like he's creating something new each time.

And he is playing the last ballade! The hardest piece of all. It's so exciting. Playing it on the Pleyel somehow showed him how the piece was meant to sound.

"I didn't get it until now," he tells Mr. Starek. "I thought I was playing it wrong. But now, on this piano, the whole piece makes sense to me. I can tell why Chopin wrote it this way."

Mr. Starek beams at him. "I am so proud of you, Michael. Regardless of how you fare in the competition. You have taken the time and made the effort to truly understand the music. That is something I could never have taught you. Chopin used to tell his students, 'Go your own way, do as you feel.' That is how you make the music your own. And you've done it. You've truly done it."

I'm proud of Michael, too. But the moments I still like best are the ones at the beginning of the lesson when we're alone. I'm so excited to see what Michael will do with the music, and then what I will do in response. Our duets. Does he feel the same way? I think so. He looks for me eagerly when he arrives each day, and as soon as Mr. Starek disappears, closing the door, we dive in. Sometimes I sing so loudly I am astonished that Mr. Starek and Emily don't hear me.

I think they *do* hear that something is different about Michael's playing in those first few private minutes behind the closed door. One day, when we've been working hard on the "Winter Wind" étude, Mr. Starek says, "I must tell you, Michael, when I hear you warming up, there's something very unusual about your playing. It's almost like you have extra fingers on the keys."

"Yes!" Emily agrees. "The sound is so rich and complicated."

I swell with pride, because I know what they're hearing is *me*.

"We want you to bring that to your performance," Mr. Starek

continues. "The way the music flows through you. A mistake I often see, even with the best pianists, is that they try to impose their own ego on the piece. They want to assert their own style. With you, it's the opposite. You're disappearing into the music, finding its emotional center. It gets you closer and closer to the real Chopin."

"I don't think it's me," Michael says.

I freeze. Surely he isn't going to spill the beans, after all this time? I hop backward on the branch, hiding in the foliage. But then he explains. "It's the piano."

He's right about the piano. It has changed everything about the way we sound together: the crystalline shimmer of the notes, the way the music lingers.

We are all looking at the Pleyel.

"I still want to know how old it is," Emily says. "I was talking to one of my professors about it, and he said if we can find the serial number, we should be able to figure out when it was made."

"What's a serial number?" Michael asks.

Mr. Starek rests his hand on the curved side of the piano. "It's a number that the piano manufacturer stamps into the wood—though sometimes it's handwritten—to identify this particular piano."

"My professor says the old Pleyel company records were just recently put online, copies of their actual ledgers," Emily says. "So if we can find the piano's serial number, maybe he can help me look up its age on the computer."

146

Michael jumps up. "Then let's find it! Where would it be?"

Emily turns to Mr. Starek. "It could be literally anywhere, right?"

Mr. Starek nods. "Yes, but there are some common places. Often it's on the back of the fallboard."

I have never heard of this thing called a fallboard, but Michael immediately scrambles onto his knees on the bench. He leans over the piano, his hands on the long, flat board behind the keys that has the little plaque with the curly letters of the Pleyel name on it.

"Can we look?" he asks.

"Not now, Michael," Mr. Starek says. "Maybe at the end of the lesson."

Michael, Emily, and I are all wilting with disappointment, but Mr. Starek remains firm. "Let's work on the last ballade. Then we'll make time to look for the serial number."

Michael sighs and settles back on the bench. He begins to play, and I hide in the bush, watching, as Mr. Starek and Emily listen carefully and make suggestions. Sometimes, Mr. Starek intercedes to play a passage himself, and I think about how there's *talent* and then there's *experience*. Mr. Starek has played this piece hundreds of times, and I can hear that in the fluid way his fingers slide from note to note, as if following a path known by heart.

Michael plays the music again and again, his concentration

intense, his fingers flying. Mr. Starek quietly makes a few comments, rarely interrupting.

Finally, as the lesson is wrapping up, Michael asks, "Please? Can we look for the serial number now?"

Mr. Starek nods. "Emily, help me lift this."

I hop out of my leafy cave to watch more closely.

Mr. Starek and Emily carefully remove the fallboard from the front of the piano and examine its length, including the paler strip of wood at its base. Even I can see that it is blank. There's no number there.

"I don't see anything. Do you?" Emily asks.

"No," Mr. Starek says. "But now that we've taken this off, let's have a closer look inside." Gently, he lays the fallboard on the floor. Then he bends over the Pleyel, peering into the dense machinery of the piano's insides.

"There are so many parts," Michael says.

"Yes," Mr. Starek tells him. "More than ten thousand pieces. Imagine the patience and care it took to build one of these."

Emily leans over with her cell phone, casting light across the gleaming strings and sturdy little hammers that somehow, miraculously, make a sound when a key is struck.

"Shine your light over here, along the spine," Mr. Starek says. I see from his gesture that he means the long, straight side of the grand piano. Even the word makes the piano seem like a living creature, an animal with a body and a backbone.

"There!" Emily says. "What's that?"

They cluster around the open front of the piano, blocking my view. I have to hop down to the windowsill to see…which I do, and when I do, my heart pounds.

There, on the inside of the long board that forms the spine of the piano, is a small, crisp black number, stamped on the wood.

"That's it!" Michael cries excitedly.

"I can't read it," Mr. Starek says. "It's too small for my old eyes."

"I can," Emily tells him. Her voice rises triumphantly. "Nine-one-six-four."

"Yes!" Michael shouts. "Now we can find out how old it is!"

"Well," Mr. Starek cautions, "only if there's a record of this particular serial number. But if Emily is willing to do a little research, maybe we can learn more."

The lesson is at an end, but I know that something else is just beginning. We have found a clue! A clue to the mystery of this old piano.

20

New Arrivals

After the lesson, I fly home, and I am just beginning my descent to the holly tree when Sebastian and Oliver meet me in midair, flapping madly around me.

"Where have you been?" Sebastian demands.

"We've been looking for you everywhere!" Oliver adds.

"I was at Michael's piano lesson," I tell them.

Sebastian eyes me suspiciously. "We looked for you by the music room. Nobody was there."

Gulp. "Today the lesson was at Mr. Starek's sister's house," I say hurriedly. "It's close by."

"You're always with that boy," Sebastian complains. "And you know what? Big things are happening while you're gone."

"What things?" I look from one brother to the other. And then I know. "The eggs?"

"They're not eggs anymore," Oliver tells me, and my brothers fly on either side of me, flanking me as I swoop down to the nest.

Mother is huddled in the center, her golden wings folded at her sides. At first, everything looks the same. But when she shifts position, I see that the pale blue eggs are gone.

In their place are three small, scrawny, wrinkly, writhing lumps. They are a dull gray color with splotches of pink, and strange tufts of pale, spiky hair stick out of their skin. Their eyes are dark and bulbous, and as soon as Mother stands, they all start opening their wide pink mouths and crying.

They are hideous.

"Mirabelle!" Mother says. "Finally, you're here." She is glowing with happiness. "Meet your three sisters."

Three sisters! What?!

"Can you believe it?" Sebastian says glumly. "Not a single boy."

"But Mother says Sebastian and I still get to name two of them," Oliver insists.

Sebastian and Ollie can name all three of them for all I care.

"What do you think?" Mother asks me.

I struggle to find something nice to say. "They look very... hungry."

"Oh yes, they're always hungry," Mother says proudly.

Sebastian lands next to me on the edge of the nest. "Aren't they the ugliest things you ever saw?"

"Sebastian!" Mother scolds him. "I told you, this is exactly how you three looked when you hatched."

None of us believe her. We think she's just trying to make excuses for these new, ugly babies.

Also, three sisters? How did *that* happen? I've been the only girl for so long. The only sister to my brothers. Now they have *four* sisters, and I'm just one of them.

"You know what would be a big help?" Mother is saying.

Of course we want to help Mother—she does so much for us—but we are all worried she's going to ask us to babysit these horrific little monsters.

"Um…what?" Sebastian asks nervously.

"Could you all gather some dandelion seeds? It's time for me to feed them again."

Phew! Anything to get out of here, away from these space aliens.

"Yes, Mother," we say as we fly away from the nest.

Mother calls, "And think of some good names for your sisters!"

It is all too much.

There's a patch of dandelions in the sun by Mr. Starek's garden shed, so we go there first. Most of the flowers have turned to downy fluff, and those are the ones with the seeds.

"Oliver, you be the lookout," Sebastian orders.

We always have to be alert for any sign of that evil old cat, Harmony, stalking around the yard.

"I'll go first," Oliver grumbles, "but then we take turns." He perches on the wisteria vine, several feet above us, amid its dry, faded blooms.

I land on one of the soft dandelion stalks. It bends toward the grass.

"When did the eggs hatch?" I ask Ollie.

"Oh, a while ago," he says. "The pecking and cracking started right after you left."

"Three *girls*," Sebastian mutters.

"Mother seems happy," I say.

"Oh yeah," Sebastian says. "She's thrilled. I don't get it. Did you see those babies? They look like they fell off the ugly tree and hit every branch on the way down."

Sebastian can only say things like this when Mother's not in earshot to stop him.

Oliver sighs. "Mother says that's just because they're brand-new. She says in another week, they'll look more like birds."

Sebastian shudders. "That will take more than a week."

Now I am feeling a little sorry for the hideous babies. "What names are you thinking of?" I ask my brothers.

"Gladiola," says Oliver.

Sebastian bursts out laughing.

"It's a flower!" Oliver protests. "Flower names are nice."

Flower names *are* nice, but I'm not sure I would have chosen Gladiola.

Sebastian snorts. "It's too long. What are we going to call her for short?"

"Glady. Or Glad," Oliver says. "Glad is nice, too, because it means 'happy.' What's your idea, anyway?"

"Something that starts with S, like my name," Sebastian says. "Maybe Serena."

Oliver and I both want Sebastian to propose a name we can make fun of, but of course he comes up with something we like.

Oliver nods grudgingly. "That's good. What about you, Mirabelle? What name are you thinking of?"

It had seemed so exciting to name the babies when Mother first

suggested it, but my enthusi-
asm is gone, even for the first
name I thought of, Annabelle. Now
I'm not sure I want any of those babies
to have a name like mine. "I don't know.
I have to think about it some more," I mumble.

"Well, you'd better hurry up. Mother wants to start calling them something," Sebastian says.

"Get the dandelion seeds," Oliver orders. "So we can have some fun before the day is over. These babies are already a lot of work."

Sebastian and I gather the tiny brown dandelion seeds in our beaks, spitting out their fluffy white tails. When my mouth is full, I swap places with Oliver, and he dutifully pecks away at a dandelion head, while I keep an eye out for danger.

There's no more conversation on our way back to the nest, because our mouths are stuffed with seeds.

"Wonderful!" Mother says when she sees us. The babies are cheeping madly. Their open pink mouths look bigger than their bodies. Mother takes some of the seeds and swallows them, then spits them up directly into the babies' gaping mouths.

"Gross," Sebastian whispers to me, but we know this is how mother birds always feed their babies. The hard seeds have to be softened and digested a little bit before the babies are able to eat them.

The babies swallow hungrily, then open their beaks again, demanding more.

When Mother finishes, she turns to us. "What about names? Did you think of any?"

"Serena," Sebastian says smugly.

"Oh, I like that very much," Mother says. She nudges one of the grotesque little aliens and says, "Here's Serena."

"I thought of Gladiola," Oliver says hesitantly. "But is it too long?"

"Not at all," Mother tells him. "That's a beautiful name. Gladiola flowers are so tall and elegant."

Oliver shoots a triumphant glance at Sebastian.

Sebastian rolls his eyes. "'Glad' is a goofy nickname."

Oliver glowers at him. "Well, the other name I thought of is Halina. Lina, for short."

Oh, I wish I'd thought of that!

Mother smiles approvingly. "Isn't that a lovely idea, in memory of the old man's sister. I think the world could use another Halina." She gently prods the second baby with her beak. "Little Lina."

"And what about you, Mirabelle?" she asks, smoothing the

spiky crest of another hatchling. "What name did you think of?"

I look at the last little baby, with its gray reptilian skin and its wing bones sticking out. It deserves a good name, too. Something strong and interesting.

"What about George?" I say. I think how George Sand wanted a name that would set her free.

Now Sebastian and Oliver are both laughing so hard they topple over and have to hang upside down.

"That's a BOY name," Sebastian roars.

"That's no good for a girl," Oliver exclaims.

"It's good for some girls," I protest. "Like George Sand! Ever heard of her? I guess you don't know as much as you think you do. She was a famous writer in France in the 1800s."

Mother smiles at me. "It's a fine name, an artistic name. I think it means she'll have an interesting life."

So there they are: Serena, Halina, and George. And already the babies don't look quite so ugly, because now they have names.

21

A Discovery

All of a sudden, we are at the end of August, and the lazy days of summer seem to be winding down. I feel like I can hardly catch my breath, between helping Mother with the new babies, gathering nuts and seeds with Ollie and Sebastian, rushing to Halina's house for piano lessons, and helping Michael prepare for the Chopin Festival. I have never been this busy in my life! I used to think only grown-up birds were busy, and I felt sorry for them, with no time to play or pretend or goof off. Who wants to live that way? Now that's how it is for me, rushing from one thing to the next.

"You're no fun anymore," Sebastian complains. "Every time we finish helping with the babies, you take off."

"I know," I say, sorry. "But I have to be at Michael's piano lessons! We're a team."

"No, *we're* a team," Sebastian says. "That boy is a human. You'd better remember that. He's never going to like you as much as he likes other humans."

Is that true? I think of our duets. Sebastian is wrong. I know in my bones that I'm the only one who can sing what Michael plays. I'm the only one who could possibly keep up! And it's helping him get better and better. I know it is.

I have to admit, the last ballade is still giving us some trouble. The two other pieces—the prelude and the "Winter Wind" étude—we do well. Why, I could sing them in my sleep! (Actually, I think I sometimes *do* sing them in my sleep, because Mother said to me one morning, "I heard you singing the strangest tune last night. It sounded so sad it gave me a chill.") But the ballade is very, very difficult. I can see why Mr. Starek calls it one of the most challenging piano pieces ever written. I'm not talking about the beginning, which Michael and I figured out long ago, though the slower pace takes a great deal of control on my part. It's the part where the piece becomes fast and loud. The finger work it requires is so quick and complex that Michael sometimes stumbles, and he isn't used to making mistakes.

"I can't get it right," he protests to Mr. Starek, his face red with frustration. "Maybe I should play the first ballade instead. I know that one."

Mr. Starek stays calm. "There's a point like this with any difficult piece," he says gently, "when it seems that you will never master it."

"But what if I don't?" Michael wails. "What if it's just a waste of time?"

Mr. Starek coughs a few times, covering his mouth with a handkerchief. I watch him closely. He has been coughing more lately, and it reminds me of the terrible cough he had in the spring. Halina's house is so full of dust, with a damp, moldy odor. I know it's been bothering him, and it worries me.

He folds the handkerchief and tucks it neatly in his pocket, like a letter into an envelope. "Learning something new is never a waste of time," he tells Michael. "And the greatest frustration often precedes the greatest breakthrough. As the saying goes, the lowest ebb of the tide is also its turning point."

But Michael is grumpy and refuses to be reassured. "Where's Emily? Why didn't she come today?"

I have been wondering the same thing myself. Emily never misses a lesson. It doesn't feel the same without her, and I think her absence partly accounts for Michael's bad mood. That, and the pressure he's feeling about the competition. We are working so hard, and the only thing we've learned is that the last ballade's impossible reputation is deserved.

"She said she would be late," Mr. Starek says.

"What's she doing?" Michael complains.

Before Mr. Starek can answer, we hear the front door open and then Emily's quick footsteps in the hallway.

She rushes into the study. "I found the piano!" she cries triumphantly. "My professor helped me search the Pleyel company records online, and I found number nine-one-six-four!"

I almost topple off my branch. She did it!

Mr. Starek gasps. "Really? You found the serial number for this piano?"

Michael leaps up from the piano bench. "How old is it?" he cries.

"You won't even believe this." Emily's cheeks are flushed.

She looks from Michael to Mr. Starek, barely able to contain herself. When she speaks, her voice is scarcely louder than a whisper. "It was made in 1842," she breathes. "It's from the time of—"

"Chopin!" Michael shouts.

22

Valuables

None of us can believe it. Eighteen hundred and forty-two?! It's almost two hundred years old. It's the same piano, but we all look at it differently now. Mr. Starek touches the glossy lid with one hand.

"So this very piano could have been sitting in one of the salons where Chopin gave a concert," he says, his voice hushed.

"Yes!" Emily cries. "What if it was played by Chopin himself?"

Michael stands up straighter and his entire attention is focused on the Pleyel. "Is that possible? Do you think it was?"

Mr. Starek shakes his head. "Wouldn't that be amazing? If you've been playing the last ballade on a piano touched by Chopin himself?"

We are all speechless, until Mr. Starek says, "But I'm sure it would have been snapped up by a museum or a collector if that were the case." He turns to Emily. "Could you tell from the company ledgers who the owner was?"

Emily shook her head. "No, unfortunately. Sometimes serial numbers were followed by the name and address where the piano was shipped, but for this one, it was just the year it was made."

Michael sits down at the piano bench, resting his hands on his knees. "Isn't there some way to figure out who it belonged to?"

Mr. Starek contemplates this. "If Halina were here, we could at least ask how she acquired it, and maybe trace its ownership history that way. But it wouldn't take us back two hundred years. It's a stroke of luck to find the serial number listed in the Pleyel records. At least we know its age."

"But not whether Chopin ever played it." Michael sounds crestfallen. Even through the window I can feel the weight of his disappointment.

"Let's pretend he did," Emily says. "Because he could have."

"And regardless," Mr. Starek adds, "you're playing a piano that sounds exactly the way Chopin's would have, the way the music would have sounded to his ear. That's the important thing."

Michael cheers up at that thought. "I want to try the ballade again," he says to Mr. Starek.

"Good," Mr. Starek says.

They are just getting started when there is a knock at the door.

At first I think it's Michael's mother, coming to hear him play, but the knock is so sharp and loud, crisp with authority, that I decide it must be a stranger.

Mr. Starek frowns. "Get started, Michael. I'll just see who that is."

When he leaves the room, Michael doesn't start playing. He and Emily strain to hear what's happening in the other room. I have a better way of finding out: I fly around the corner of the house to the front porch.

There are two men in suits standing on the rough wood boards.

"Hello, Mr. Starek," the thin, gray man says, and I recognize him: that fellow from the bank who came to Mr. Starek's house a few weeks ago, the one who reminded me of a tufted titmouse.

Mr. Starek says, "Mr. Popinski, isn't it?" His face takes on a wary expression. "May I help you?"

Mr. Popinski sounds slightly apologetic. "I wasn't expecting to find you here. We've come to secure the house."

"Excuse me?" Mr. Starek looks puzzled.

"Unfortunately, we were unable to grant another extension on the loan." He speaks rapidly, beckoning Mr. Starek onto the porch with him.

Michael and Emily appear in the doorway, looking startled.

"I did advocate for you with the loan department," he continues, "but the account is seriously in arrears. Your sister owed a great deal of money. I'm afraid we had to pursue an order from the probate court, allowing us to sell the house. The bank will be taking possession of the property."

"You mean a foreclosure?" Mr. Starek sounds alarmed. "I had hoped to avoid that."

"Yes, we all did," Mr. Popinski says. "We certainly tried."

I can see that the other man is edging his way into the house, past Emily and Michael, who watch him in bewilderment.

Mr. Popinski shakes his head. "But as you're unable to pay off the outstanding debt and associated fees, there's no other option, I'm afraid."

I can see the distress on Mr. Starek's face, the crisscross of worry lines. "May I at least have time to deal with my sister's things? It's been rather overwhelming, you see...."

"Yes, I can see that," Mr. Popinski says, glancing into the house and wrinkling his nose in distaste. "Quite a lot of clutter."

Clutter! My feathers bristle. Sure, Halina's house is full of too many things, but they're not clutter. They were valuable, and treasured by her—we know that now.

The other man has slipped inside Halina's house and is moving swiftly through it. He seems to be taking pictures using a small computer and then typing notes.

What is going on?

"Could I have more time to sort this out?" Mr. Starek asks again.

"I'm sorry, Mr. Starek, that isn't possible. Your sister's debt is so large that the bank has placed a lien against all the estate's assets. The lien was granted by the probate court this morning... which is why I'm here."

Who can understand what he's talking about? None of these words are familiar, but it seems to mean that these people from the bank are taking over Halina's house. Mr. Popinski hands Mr. Starek a folder full of papers.

"What's a lien?" Michael asks, his eyes wide.

But Mr. Popinski is already moving toward the door. "This will explain everything, including your rights at this juncture."

We are all trying to comprehend what's happening. Emily steps forward, her eyes panicked. "The estate's assets? You don't mean what's in the house, do you?"

Mr. Popinski walks past her, his hand on the front doorknob. "The contents, yes. The bank will be selling the house and any valuables. It's a regrettable situation, but given the circumstances, Mr. Starek, this is the only way to settle your sister's significant debts."

Now I understand. The bank is taking the house and everything in it! That means the piano—the Pleyel piano, the piano from 1842.

"But does this have to be done right now?" I hear the note of desperation in Mr. Starek's voice.

"Unfortunately, yes. I'm terribly sorry, but I have to ask you and the children to leave the premises."

Emily's face flushes, and I think it's from both the situation and him calling her a child. "This isn't fair," she says.

Mr. Popinski is already inside the house. "Again, I am sorry, but you all need to leave. We'll be installing locks on the doors this afternoon. No one but the bank's representatives will be permitted to enter."

With that grim pronouncement, he closes the door in our faces.

"What are we going to do?" Michael cries, turning to Mr. Starek. "The piano!"

"I know, I know," Mr. Starek says. "I'll contact the probate court. Maybe they can intercede." But even to me, his voice sounds hopeless.

Michael turns to Emily in distress. "I need to keep playing it. I'm almost ready."

"You are," Emily says fiercely. "We have to figure something out."

"But you heard what he said. They're putting locks on the doors!" Michael sounds like he's trying not to cry. "What if I can't ever play the Pleyel again?"

Emily bends close to his face, whispering, "We'll find a way. We have to."

Mr. Starek turns toward the street. "I...I just thought I had more time. Emily, call Michael's mother, will you? Let her know that we're finishing the lesson at my house. We'll have to practice there tomorrow."

He steps off the porch and walks toward his car, head down-cast, coughing into his handkerchief.

23

All Locked Up

When I get back to the nest that afternoon, the babies are cheeping loudly, and Mother is patiently feeding them, one at a time. They do look a bit better every day. The fragile pink color is fading, and the gray spikes of hair are turning into tufts of feathers. Sebastian and Oliver are nowhere in sight.

"Your brothers are at the bird feeder," Mother tells me, but the words are barely out of her beak before Sebastian comes torpedoing into the holly tree, followed by Oliver.

The branches shake, and I nearly fall off my perch.

"Boys!" Mother reprimands. "You'll scare the babies."

"It was a race," Sebastian says. "And I won."

"That's because you took off before I said 'Go,'" Oliver protests.

"Stop," I tell them before it turns into a full-blown fight. "I have a problem."

I need to talk about what is happening with the piano! It is so upsetting. But I can't tell them everything. They don't know about my duets with Michael. They do know that I watch his piano lessons, and they know the lessons have moved to Halina's house, on the other side of the river.

Mother looks at me sharply. "What's the matter? You've been gone so much lately, Mirabelle. We miss you! I think you're spending too much time with the humans."

"But, Mother, Mr. Starek is in trouble," I say.

I decide to start there, because Mother is fond of Mr. Starek.

The babies begin their shrill, squeaky cries again, but Mother shushes them. "Why?" she asks.

"What's happened?" Oliver demands.

"Yeah, spit it out," Sebastian says. "We'll help."

I take a deep breath. "You know how we've been going to his sister's house for Michael to practice on her special piano? Well, Halina owed a lot of money to the bank, and today people from the bank came and kicked us out. And they're locking up her house, with everything in it."

"Oh, that is terrible," Mother says. "That must be very distressing for Mr. Starek."

"It is!" I say. "But it's worse than that: if the bank locks up the house, Michael won't be able to practice on her Pleyel piano.

171

And he has been playing so well, getting ready for the festival."

Sebastian snorts. "Why can't he just play the piano at the old man's house? That's the one he was using before anyway."

Mother nods in agreement. "That seems a sensible alternative. It is the piano all the other students used, when they were preparing for competitions. And some of them did very well, didn't they?"

"But—" I begin. How can I explain it to them? "This piano is different," I say finally. "Michael is playing better than he ever has. Emily did some research and we just found out that it's a really old piano—it was made when *Chopin* was alive." Do they understand how important this is? "It's helping Michael play the music exactly the way Chopin wanted it to be played," I finish feebly. It doesn't sound convincing even to me.

Mother, Sebastian, and Oliver are all silent.

"So you need a way to get into Halina's house," Oliver says finally.

"Yes!" I feel a twinge of hope.

"We can get into the house," Sebastian says. "We can get into *any* house."

My spirits are lifting. My brothers are going to help me. "But even if we get in, we need to find a way for Michael to get in," I tell them.

"Now, wait a minute," Mother says. "I know you want to help him, Mirabelle, but you mustn't take unnecessary risks. If the house has been locked up by the bank, I'm not sure it's safe for you to be there."

"Well…" I say. "There's nobody living in it."

"Yeah," Sebastian says. "It's probably safer than hanging around *this* house, with the old man and the cat."

I turn to Mother. "Could they come with me to have a look?" I beg. "Please?"

"It's too late today," Mother says firmly.

"What about tomorrow?" Oliver asks, and I shoot him a grateful glance. As much as they tease and annoy me, when I am in trouble, I can always count on my brothers. We are in this together.

Mother turns back to the babies. "We'll see."

We'll see is one of the most dreaded parental pronouncements ever. It's usually a delay tactic until Mother can think of a good enough reason to say no, or until we forget what we were begging to do, or until another interesting possibility presents itself and we move on. But this time we are not about to forget or give up.

The very next morning, we start begging her again.

"Please, Mother," I say. "Michael's lesson is this afternoon! We don't have much time."

"We'll all stay together," Sebastian volunteers.

"And be super careful," Ollie chimes in.

Mother is distracted with the babies and I can tell that she's tired of the back-and-forth with us. "I don't want you to do anything foolhardy," she says.

Hooray! She's relenting.

"Watch out for each other," she warns us. "And come straight back here at the first sign of trouble."

"Yes, Mother," we promise.

The summer day is hazy and hot. As soon as we've cleared the holly tree, I ask my brothers, "Are you ready to break into Halina's house?" I figure the mission will seem more enticing if there's a bit of lawlessness to it.

Oliver says, "Sure!" And Sebastian says, "Let's do it."

I soar up over the neat green square of Mr. Starek's backyard, with its bright flower patches and thick shrubbery, and my brothers follow. We fly over rooftops and patios and neatly tended vegetable gardens, over quiet streets and busy roads and finally the wide, glistening ribbon of river. Then we're in the neighborhood where Halina lives. I dip down toward the sagging roof of her house.

"Wow," Sebastian says, landing on the splintery porch railing. "What a dump."

"There's been nobody living here," I say. "That's why things are falling apart." I feel strangely protective of Halina. She's not here to defend herself.

Ollie wears a dubious expression. "It looks like they've been falling apart for a long time," he says.

I flutter over to the front door. There's a new black lockbox over the knob, and a metal brace with a padlock screwed to the frame. Nobody's going to get in this way.

"Okay." Sebastian takes charge, as usual. "Let's fly around the outside and see if there are any openings."

The air is heavy with late summer smells, the sweet scent of roses and lilies, the grassy odor of mown lawns. I fly first to the study window. It's always open so that Michael and I can hear each other. Maybe the men from the bank forgot to close it?

But no, when I land in the rhododendron near the dusty windowpanes, I can see that the window is shut tight. That's discouraging, because it means those men from the bank went through the house thoroughly.

Above me, I can see Ollie and Sebastian wheeling around the second story. After a minute, they drop down to the shrubbery and land next to me.

"It's locked up tight," Oliver declares.

"Really? There's no way in?" This is a disaster. The festival is soon! We've made so much progress, so many plans. I am beginning to feel despondent.

Sebastian snorts. "Who said that? There's always a way in. Let's go down the chimney."

Oliver and I look at each other. We know what Mother would think of that idea. Chimneys are dark, sooty, and dangerous. There are many stories of birds getting stuck in them, flapping around aimlessly to their doom. And there can be all sorts of other creatures in chimneys—squirrels, raccoons, possums. Halina's house has been abandoned for many months. Why wouldn't some animal have taken up residence in the chimney?

"What if there's something living in there?" I ask.

"That's mostly in winter, when it's cold outside and the chimney's warm," Sebastian says. "Besides, we're faster than any old thing that could be living down there. If we see anything bigger than us, we'll fly back up."

"What if that metal flap over the fireplace is shut?" Ollie asks. "Then we won't be able to get into the house anyway."

"Yeah," I say. "The damper."

Sebastian is undaunted. "Well, we won't know until we take a look. What, are you guys chicken?"

Of course we're not! That makes us so mad that Ollie and I fly up to the chimney fast-fast-fast, and get there before Sebastian does. It's like a game of Flight Club.

The top of the chimney is a jumble of crooked bricks, chipped and missing the mortar in between. It is pitch-black inside, and it smells like ash.

Are we really going down this thing?

24

The Way In

I'm nervous, but I can't think of a better idea. Oliver and I are perched on the edge of the chimney, trying to decide what to do, when suddenly Sebastian barrels straight past us into the darkness. He disappears.

Yikes!

I peer into the void and see his bright yellow wings swallowed up by the black hole.

"Hellooooooooooooo," I call, leaning over the crumbling brick rim. "Sebastian! Is it safe?"

He chirps a few times distantly. "Yep! And the damper's open. I'm inside the house. Come on!"

Oliver and I look at each other.

"You first," Ollie says.

I take a deep breath and glide down, down, down into the blackness, trying not to breathe. I can feel the stale, sooty air stirring behind me as Ollie follows.

Sebastian is right: the damper is open. A weak patch of light brightens the bottom of the chimney. I swoop out into Halina's living room.

It is as dusty and crowded as I remembered, with pieces of furniture jammed against each other and boxes stacked in precarious towers, overflowing with her collection of things. Those bank people certainly didn't bother to clean anything up.

Sebastian is gripping the arm of a wall lamp, looking around. Oliver lands on a coatrack. "Why is it such a mess?" he asks.

I hesitate. It's Halina's house and this is just the way she lived.

I shrug my wings. "I think she never threw anything away."

"I guess not!" Sebastian says, disgusted. "It's going to be hard for us to even fly around in here. Forget about finding a way for the boy to get inside."

"But we have to," I protest. "The competition is only two weeks away! He needs the Pleyel piano. You don't understand."

"All right, stop the waterworks," Sebastian snaps, which is annoying because I'm not crying. I'm just trying to explain why we need to find a way for Michael to get in.

"Go upstairs and see if anything's open," he tells me. "Oliver, check out that room over there. I'll take this big room."

Sebastian is so bossy! He's never been in this house before, but already he is full of ideas for what we should be doing, and ordering everybody around. Oliver obediently disappears through the archway into the dining room, where the big chandelier hangs from the middle of the ceiling.

As I am flying over the banister and up the dark staircase. Oliver yells, "Hey! There's another bird in here!" And then, "It's flying straight at me. HELP!"

What?! Another bird in the house?

"I hope it's not an owl," Sebastian says, alarmed. An owl would make a nice feast of the three of us.

Sebastian and I immediately zoom through the archway, and find Oliver fluttering wildly in front of a wall, inches away from a bright yellow goldfinch that looks just like him.

"That's a mirror, you goofball." Sebastian bursts out laughing.

Ollie retreats sheepishly from his reflection and lands on the spindled back of an old chair. "Oh," he says. "It's hard to tell when it's so dark in here."

"Didn't you recognize yourself?" Sebastian demands, incredulous.

Oliver is annoyed. "Well, I did think it was a really good-looking bird."

I try to make him feel better. "At least you didn't bang your head."

Mother has told us stories of birds flying into their reflections in windows or mirrors, thinking they're being attacked by another bird that looks just like them. Sometimes they knock themselves out or, worse yet, die from the impact.

"Yeah," Oliver agrees, but Sebastian is still laughing when I leave them to explore upstairs.

The second floor of Halina's house is even worse than the downstairs, packed to the bursting point with furniture, racks of clothing, and row upon row of framed pictures stacked against the walls. But at least there's more light up here. The curtains are open in most of the rooms, and beams of sunlight shine through the dirty windowpanes.

I fly from window to window, looking out at the overgrown yard. The windows are all shut tight. There isn't so much as a broken windowpane to offer a way in. This is hopeless! Will Michael never have another chance to play the Pleyel?

"How's it looking up there?" Oliver shouts from down below.

"All the windows are locked," I say, demoralized. "There's no way in."

I'm about to fly back down to join my brothers when something catches my eye. Resting against the wall of one of the bedrooms is a large, framed oil painting, and unlike the other paintings and photographs, which are stacked haphazardly and leaning against one another, this painting is turned to face the room.

I'm not sure I would have noticed it otherwise. It's big, and bordered by an ornately carved wooden frame, covered in chipped flecks of gold.

It's a painting of a piano. A grand piano made of beautiful red-brown wood, with an unmistakable pattern of ripples and waves that gleam in lustrous swirls. There are a couple of brass florets on the side.

I catch my breath.

It's the piano in the study! It's a painting of the Pleyel.

To be fair, it's not the whole piano. It's angled away from the viewer so that you can't even see the keys. The background of the painting is a vibrant bronze color, rich brown mottled with red and orange and gold. There are thick black brushstrokes creating a wedge of darkness in front of the piano. On the top near the music rack is a small vase of flowers, a vivid patch of bright colors.

But I would recognize it anywhere. I know it's the Pleyel. The pattern of the wood is so distinctive. I see the wave. I even see the darker shape that looks like a lily pad.

"Hey!" I call to Sebastian and Oliver. "Come look at this."

They swoop into the room and land on the open drawer of a dresser.

"Ugh," Sebastian says. "The upstairs is just as crammed with junk as the downstairs."

"It's not junk," I say. Halina must have loved these things, her belongings, the keepsakes of a lifetime. "Look what I found."

Oliver tilts his bright yellow head to one side, and I think his black crest looks like a rakish little beret. He studies the painting curiously, but Sebastian is impatient.

"Big deal. It's a picture of a piano."

And then I remember that they know nothing of the Pleyel downstairs; they haven't even seen it yet.

"It's the piano in the study downstairs," I say. "The one Michael has been playing. It's really, really old."

The brushstrokes in the painting catch the sunlight, and I see cracks and ridges in the thick oil paint.

Sebastian shrugs. "I don't know, but what I do know is, we're wasting time! These windows are locked. We need to find some other way for that boy to get inside."

He flaps into the air and soars out of the room.

"Come on," Ollie says. "We have to go home soon. You can look at the picture later."

I know my brothers are right. If we don't get out of here soon, I'll be late for Michael's piano lesson, and I have never been late for a lesson. I just can't be, because then he'll have to warm up without me.

Reluctantly, I turn away from the oil painting. Could Halina have made this painting of her Pleyel? Why would anyone paint a piano and not show the keys? It is all very mysterious.

25

A Door in the Door

The three of us fly through the rooms of the first floor, window to window, confirming what we already know: everything is locked tight.

"Maybe we could break a window," Oliver suggests.

Sebastian scoffs, "How would we do that? By flying into it? That's the worst idea ever."

It's true. Too many birds meet terrible fates flying into windows they never realized were there.

"What are we going to do?" I am filled with despair.

"Whatever we do, it has to be soon," Oliver says. "Look outside."

The sunny day has changed. One part of the sky is still blue, but the other part is dark with a mass of purply-gray clouds. I can see the trees swaying with gusts of wind.

I fly into the study and, sure enough, the window by the piano is not just shut, but locked. Then into the kitchen. All the windows there are locked, too. There's a door to a small, screened porch, but it's also locked.

And then I see something I hadn't noticed before.

In the base of the door that leads to the screened porch, cut out of the wood, is a metal-rimmed rectangular opening covered by a rubber flap. I don't think it's a cat door, because it's bigger than the one at Mr. Starek's house, for dreadful old Harmony. It must be for a dog?

Yikes! I am briefly horrified at the thought that Halina might have had a cat or a dog that nobody knew about, but then I remember we've been in the house a dozen times and never seen or heard anything. Plus, this little pet door looks old. Really old. Like it hasn't been used by anything in years and years. Now, mind you, it is a small door, certainly not people-size. But Michael is small. Could he possibly squeeze through it?

I can see through the window that the screened porch door is also latched. It has one of those metal hooks holding it shut. But I'm pretty sure Sebastian, Ollie, and I can find a way to get that open if we put our minds to it.

"Hey!" I yell to my brothers. "Come help me!"

They're there in an instant, gliding around the kitchen. "Oh!" Ollie says. "Look at the little door."

"Can you get that rubber thing open?" Sebastian asks.

"I think so," I say, "but it's going to be heavy."

We all drop down to the floor, examining the edge of the rubber flap. The door is clearly designed to swing both ways, so whatever animal once used it could go in and out.

"Let's try to push it open," Sebastian proposes.

We line up, three in a row, gripping the lower metal rim of the pet door. We butt our heads against the rubber flap simultaneously. It's heavy! But it swings just a smidgen into the screened porch, and we all flap and tumble through the opening onto the rough porch floor.

It's cooler on the porch. The sky is fully dark now, and the wind has picked up.

"There should be a doggy door here, too," Sebastian says. "So the dog could get out into the yard."

He's right, but when we look around, there are screens on all sides of us.

"Maybe somebody closed it up," Ollie says.

"Or maybe the porch wasn't here when the dog was," I say.

The porch, like the rest of the house, is falling apart, and the screens have small rips and gashes in them, and some big, wrinkled areas that have been patched.

"Help me undo the hook on the door," I say. "Then I can show Michael the way in."

"I've got it," Sebastian says. He joins me above the door handle, where a rusty hook latches into a small metal ring. We both grip it with our claws.

"Now," Sebastian says.

I tug with all my might. The hook doesn't budge.

"Again," Sebastian orders.

We try as best we can, but we aren't strong enough to get the hook out of the ring. Ugh.

Then I have an idea.

"What if we make a hole in the screen right here, next to the hook, so Michael can reach his fingers in and unlatch it?"

188

"Sure," Sebastian says. "There are so many holes in this screen already. What's one more?"

He and I begin pecking and clawing at the loose panel of screen next to the hook, until we've torn a hole in it. I spit out bits of metal mesh. *Blech!*

"Michael can fit his hand through that," I tell my brothers, ecstatic. "Now he'll be able to get into the house and play the piano!"

"I still don't see why that matters so much," Sebastian says. "But yeah, as long as he can squeeze through that doggy door, he can get in."

"We did it!" Oliver shouts, just as a clap of thunder shatters the August afternoon.

"I told you we would," Sebastian scoffs. "Now let's GO, before the storm hits."

We briefly debate going back up the chimney, but Sebastian points out that our hole in the screen is big enough for us to fit through if we're careful. I go first, since I know the way home best, squeezing past the torn mesh and soaring into the sky. The wind is really blowing now, and I can barely keep my balance. A strong gust sweeps me back toward the house.

"Do you think we should wait it out?" Oliver calls. He's being blown off course, too, knocked around by the wind.

Here's the thing about storms: birds never fly in them. The

wind is too strong for us to stay on course, and a heavy rain can drench our feathers and send us plummeting to the ground. We know better than to perch at the top of tall trees, because that's where lightning can strike. So what we'll usually do is settle ourselves on a thick branch close to the trunk of a tree or bush, on the side most protected from the rain and the wind, and wait till the storm is over.

That's what we should be doing now. I know it. But I can't miss Michael's piano lesson! And we told Mother we'd come back to the nest soon. She'll worry if the weather gets bad and we're not safely home.

"We can make it," Sebastian urges. "Just keep going."

As the rain begins to pelt from the heavy, glowering sky, I try my best to fly in a straight line, leading Oliver and Sebastian over the dark rooftops and empty backyards toward Mr. Starek's house.

The rain falls faster and faster.

A flash of lightning streaks jaggedly above us, and then:

BOOM!

A deafening clap of thunder shakes the air.

I am buffeted by the rain and the wind, whipped back and forth. I can barely see, and as hard as I'm trying to flap my wings, I can tell I'm about to be dashed to the ground.

"Mirabelle!" I hear Oliver's voice far behind me.

Panicking, I fly into the dense branches of a lilac bush, which is shuddering violently in the wind.

I can't see either of my brothers, only the driving rain, falling in sheets, flooding the pavement and soaking the lawns.

"Oliver!" I call. "Sebastian!"

26

Storm

The rain is so thick the air seems to have become a solid thing. Where are my brothers? All I can see are the blurry shapes of trees, the shadowy peaks of houses.

"Sebastian!" I scream. "Oliver!"

And then I glimpse something else, a speck of brilliant yellow, rocketing through the rain.

"Mirabelle, help!" It's Oliver.

"Here!" I shout. "I'm in the lilac bush!"

He is flying so low to the ground now I think

he's going to crash. Abruptly, the wind sweeps him up, and I'm afraid he's going to be blown into the side of a house.

"Ollie, over here! Do you see me? By the fence."

And then he does see me, and in a spinning, tumbling, flapping frenzy, he careens into the lilac bush.

I hop quickly to him, pressing my body against his, smoothing his soaked feathers with my beak. "Are you okay?"

We huddle close for warmth.

"I lost Sebastian!" Oliver wails. "He was behind me, and then he wasn't."

"He'll be fine," I say quickly, trying to reassure us both. "Sebastian can handle anything."

We keep squinting through the gray rain, praying for a flash of yellow.

"What should we do?" Oliver asks.

I truly don't know. Should we go back and try to find Sebastian? Should we go home, where Mother will be frantic with worry? Or should we stay here in the bush, where we're safe, until the storm ends?

We can't leave Sebastian behind. But with this terrible rain and wind, I don't think we'll be able to look for him ourselves.

Mother will know what to do. We have to get back to the nest.

"We'll fly from bush to bush," I tell Oliver, "so we're not out in the open. If we only fly short distances, we can make it back to the holly tree."

"But what about Sebastian?" Oliver cries.

"We'll find Sebastian, but we need Mother's help."

Grimly, we set out for the nest. I fly as fast as I can to the top of the fence, and then to a small apple tree. It is shaking so hard in the wind that apples tumble down, smacking the ground.

I wait for Oliver, and a minute later, he catapults into the tree.

That is how we go, through torrents of rain, from tree to bush to tree, yard to yard to yard. When we get to the river, there is no way to avoid being out in the open, and the wind is blowing hard across it, driving the pellets of rain into our breasts. I try to set a course but am immediately swept sideways. I keep pushing into the wind. Finally, I reach the opposite shore. For a minute, I can't see Oliver anywhere, and I'm worried that I've lost both my brothers. But then I spot him several trees away.

We fly toward each other, and start all over again, the painful journey from perch to perch. Finally, we reach Mr. Starek's backyard.

In the green holly tree, I see Mother's golden shape in a crowd of leaves, her sharp eyes scanning the yard.

"Mirabelle! Oliver!" she shouts.

We fly to her as fast as we can.

Drenched and shivering, we are barely able to speak. "You never should have tried to fly in this storm!" Mother scolds. "It's way too dangerous. What have I told you about rainstorms?" She's peering into the downpour. "Where's Sebastian?"

"We thought you'd be worried," I say. "We were just trying to get home."

"I would have been worried, but I would have come looking for you when it was safe to fly. *Where's Sebastian?*"

She hops to the end of the branch, squinting through the rain-thick air.

"We don't know," Oliver cries. "He was with me, but the wind blew him away."

Mother shakes her head grimly. "Tell me exactly the way you came, Mirabelle. How far is Halina's house?"

I explain it to her, the path over the neighborhood yards, across the river, into the other part of town where the houses are older and farther apart.

"The roof is sagging. The yard is full of weeds. And there are big locks on all the doors—that's how you'll know it's Halina's house."

"All right," Mother says. "I'm going to look for him. You two stay with the babies. No matter what happens, you *stay right here.*"

Stay with the babies all by ourselves?

"What if they get hungry?" Oliver asks in horror.

"You know where the extra seeds are. You can feed them just like I do," Mother calls over her shoulder as she flaps off into the storm.

Oliver and I look at each other. I know we're both worried sick about Sebastian, but we're afraid to say so out loud. What has happened to him? Where could he be?

We're alone in the nest, with our three little sisters. They have feathers now, and their eyes are not as enormous and bulging as they used to be. They are staring at us expectantly, Serena, Lina, and George.

Cheep! Cheep-cheep! Cheep-cheep-cheep-cheep-cheep!

"Here they go," Oliver says morosely.

"They're probably just scared of the storm," I say. But soon enough they are opening their pink mouths wide, badgering us for food.

Distantly, I hear Emily's car in Mr. Starek's driveway, and I know Michael's piano lesson is beginning. Without me.

Ollie and I take turns sifting through the clumps of thistle-down that Mother has gathered, looking for little black seeds to feed them. We have to chew the hard seeds and regurgitate them into the babies' mouths. Yuck. As fast as the babies gobble them up, they demand more.

At least it's much warmer and drier here in the holly tree, protected by the thick foliage. I keep peeking through the leaves into the driving rain, thinking of how hard it was to fly with the storm pummeling me. Poor Sebastian!

Oliver must be thinking the same thing. "What if Mother can't find him?" he says. And then: "What if something happens to her? What if she doesn't come back?"

We stare bleakly at the babies, who have stopped their clamoring but are still watching us with bright eyes.

"We'll be stuck taking care of them," I say, feeling hopeless. I've missed Michael's piano lesson, and if something happens to Mother, I'll never get to go to another one. Or sing Chopin! The babies are so much work.

"She'll find Sebastian and she'll come back," Ollie whispers.

We wait and wait, squinting through the dark, wet leaves. I hear Emily's car start up again, and I know the lesson must have ended. For the first time since Michael started lessons with Mr. Starek, he has played the piano without me.

Finally, the rain seems to let up a bit. The steady rush tapers off to a drizzle. The sky is a slick, glistening gray, but there's still enough light to see the shapes of the fence and the shed and Mr. Starek's house, across the dark yard.

"Why aren't they here yet?" Oliver worries.

It seems so long since Sebastian, Ollie, and I were at Halina's house, trying to find a way inside.

And then I see something...a bright, shimmering yellow, pelting through the damp air.

Sebastian!

He swoops into the holly tree, landing on a branch with such force that the leaves shake and spray us with water.

"Sebastian! Sebastian, where were you?" Oliver and I cry, surrounding him. We stroke his wet feathers with our beaks, droplets streaming off him.

He looks a little shaken, but not so different from his usual self. "I was trapped!" he says. "The wind blew me into a gutter and my wing got caught in the downspout. And then you guys left me," he adds accusingly.

"We didn't mean to!" I protest. "We thought you were right behind us."

"Well, I wasn't. I was stuck in the pouring rain while you guys were here in our nice, warm tree. Thanks for nothing."

A second later, Mother flies into the holly tree and lands gracefully on the rim of the nest.

"Hooray!" Oliver shouts with relief.

The babies are thrilled to see her and immediately begin a loud chorus of chirping.

Sebastian starts to complain about us again, but Mother stops him.

"Oh, hush, Sebastian," she says. "*None* of you should have been flying in such terrible weather. I've warned you a thousand times."

"We didn't know what to do," I tell her. "We got scared."

"I realize that," Mother says, "but nobody makes a good decision out of fear." She shakes her head at us. "And we nearly lost Sebastian! The next time a storm hits, *stay where you are*. Find shelter there, and I will come get you when it's safe."

"Yes, Mother," we say, chastened.

We all settle down to roost, now that the storm has subsided and night is coming.

What a day it's been! I feel sad about Michael playing alone. I can't make a sad face with my beak, but if I could, it would look like this: :(

Oh well, I comfort myself by thinking that I found a way for him to get inside Halina's house. He can play the Pleyel again! I just have to show him. And not only the way into the house. I also want to show him the painting I found.

27

Tricks

The next day, as soon as I see Emily's car pull into Mr. Starek's driveway, I fly to the shrubbery by the front porch. Michael rushes to the door the minute he sees me, before Emily has even gotten out of the car.

"Mirabelle," he whispers. "Where *were* you? Why didn't you come to my lesson?" His face is full of such confusion and distress that I hardly know what to do.

I flutter closer to him, trying to telepathically convey my apology.

"It was awful," Michael continues, his cheeks flushed. "I kept messing up. I couldn't get anything right." His dark eyes burn into mine. "I couldn't play without you."

I am horrified. Okay, I admit, I do feel a brief thrill at this—that I matter so much to him, that he needs me to play—but it is immediately followed by a crushing wave of guilt and worry. I love our duets, but I want them to make Michael better at the piano, not worse. Not dependent on me. What if I couldn't sing without Michael there? That would be terrible.

"You can't ever do that again," he says as Emily starts up the walk. "You can't leave me like that."

Emily clangs the bell and smiles at me. "I was worried about you, Mirabelle," she says. "I'm glad you made it through that rainstorm okay."

Now, isn't that nice? She was worried about me! That's how you can tell someone likes you. Nobody spends time worrying about people they don't like.

Emily pulls the cord of the bell again, and we all listen to its loud, metallic tolling.

Michael looks at her, puzzled. "Why isn't he answering?"

"Maybe he's resting," Emily says. "He wasn't feeling well yesterday."

"I know," Michael says. "But is he too sick to answer the door?"

As they are debating this, we all hear a shuffling noise inside the house, and the door swings open.

I see immediately that Mr. Starek isn't well. He's pale, wearing his navy bathrobe. Has he not even gotten dressed today?

He takes a step backward and coughs painfully into his sleeve. It is a rough, scraping cough, like the one he had last spring, and I feel a cold stab of worry. He was so sick then.

"I'm sorry," he says. "Didn't you get my message, Michael? I'm afraid I have to cancel our lesson today. I'm not feeling well."

"Oh no," Emily says. "Did we wake you up?"

"Not at all," Mr. Starek answers. "I was just resting."

"I'm sorry we disturbed you," Emily says. "Is there anything you need?"

"No, nothing," Mr. Starek says. "You are welcome to come in and use the piano, but I wouldn't want to expose you to...whatever virus this is."

"That's okay," Michael says. "I can keep practicing at my house. It's just..." He stops, looking gloomily at the porch floor. "Do you think I'll ever get to play the Pleyel again? Are those people from the bank going to sell it?"

Mr. Starek hesitates. "I don't know," he says. "I contacted the court this morning to see if there's anything I can do to put a hold on things. Somebody is supposed to call me back."

Michael continues to stare at the stoop. "Okay," he mumbles. He raises his eyes. "I hope you feel better."

Mr. Starek looks at him closely. "Have you been working on your pieces at home, Michael?"

The boy nods.

"Don't be discouraged about yesterday. Every musician has

experienced that, a time when each note is a challenge. And I know you had a tiring day, with school starting."

That's right! Michael started sixth grade, at his new school. No wonder he seems stressed out. It makes me feel even worse about missing his lesson yesterday.

"But what if that happens to me at the festival?" Michael asks softly. "What if I just can't play?" I hear the dread in his voice.

"First of all, it won't happen," Mr. Starek says firmly. "Because you will be prepared for it. You need to train your mind as well as your fingers. I'm going to give you a few tricks to practice at home."

"What tricks?" Michael asks.

Mr. Starek steps back from the doorway and coughs into his sleeve again. His whole body shakes, and even though he's tall, he looks frail to me, like a strong wind could blow him over. Suddenly, I see the veins in his hands, the brown age spots along his hairline. I hadn't noticed them before. He coughs again, then straightens, gripping the door for support.

"Listen. The next time you practice, right before you play the piano, I want you to put your body in a physical state that mimics the stress of the performance," he tells Michael. "Do jumping jacks, run in circles, make your heart beat faster and your palms sweat, make yourself out of breath."

Michael looks bewildered, but Emily nods, her lips curving in a smile of recognition. She has clearly heard this advice before.

"Then, in that state of physical stress," Mr. Starek continues, "run to the piano, sit down, and play something easy that you know by heart. What would you play?"

"The Minute Waltz," Michael answers promptly.

"Good, the Minute Waltz," Mr. Starek says. "Play carelessly, without giving it a thought. Play with abandon."

Michael seems shocked. "But..." he begins. "I can do that at home, but I could never play that way in a competition."

"Ah," Mr. Starek says, "but that is how you will win."

He coughs, then wheezes, then steps backward into the house. "I'm afraid I need to lie down," he tells them.

Emily and Michael both look at him anxiously. "Do you need medicine?" Emily asks. "I could run to the drugstore."

"No, no, I'll be fine," Mr. Starek says. He starts to turn away. "I have faith in you, Michael. And remember: play as if you hadn't a care in the world." He pauses. "Play as if you were Chopin during one of those lazy summers in Nohant, at George Sand's house, with the fragrance of the flowers and the songs of the birds for company."

With that, he closes the door, and we can all hear his cough fading as he climbs the stairs.

"He doesn't sound good," Michael says, looking concerned. "And what are we going to do now? I need to play the Pleyel. I just have to."

Come on! I want to shout at them. *Let's go to Halina's!*

But they have to reach that conclusion themselves.

"Michael, they were locking up the house. And you heard what they said—it belongs to the bank now."

"I don't care who the house belongs to," Michael protests. "I just want to play the piano."

"I know, but how?" Emily asks.

I fly right between them, my wings fanning the air near their faces. Then I hover, flapping, a few feet above them.

They both stare at me, surprised. "What's Mirabelle doing?" Emily asks.

I zip up into the sky, then loop back to them, circling above their heads.

Michael watches me. "She wants us to follow her."

Yay, that's right!

"Really?" Emily squints up at me. "Where?"

"I bet she wants to go back to Halina's house," Michael says. "She likes that piano as much as I do."

Emily looks at him. "What do you mean? Mirabelle can't play the piano."

"No," Michael says quickly. "I just mean she likes watching me play."

I soar in a triumphant curlicue through the air above them, before dropping gently down to land on Michael's shoulder.

He jumps a little when he feels my sharp claws through his shirt, but then he turns toward me and his dark eyes are filled

with everything that lies between us. His nose is nearly touching my beak. I want to memorize everything about his face.

"See?" he says to Emily. "I was right. She's trying to tell us something. Can't we go now? Please?"

Emily is staring at me, too. "Is that what you want?" she asks, tilting her head at me. "To go to Halina's house?"

I tilt my head back at her and then hop right over to land on her arm, which is bare and warm from the sun.

"Ouch!" she says, but she laughs with delight, and I quickly soar into the sky again. Enough with these silly humans! *I* am going to Halina's house, whether they follow me or not.

I hear Michael far below. "There she goes! Come on, Emily, hurry." And I hear the familiar rumble of her car engine, and I know they're right behind me.

28

Trespassers

When I reach Halina's house, I can't help but notice there are two large white forbidding signs posted by the bank, and of course the heavy metal locks on the door. I sit on the porch railing, waiting for Michael and Emily.

Her gray sedan has barely pulled into the driveway when Michael flings the door open. He runs across the weedy yard to the front porch. "Do you see? Mirabelle's here! I told you," he shouts.

"And do you see?" Emily answers. "That door is, like, triple-locked. I told you."

I wait till I'm sure Michael is watching me, and then fly around the corner of the house toward the screened porch.

He trots right after me, calling to Emily over his shoulder.

"Let's try to get in through the window in the piano room. I left it open."

Well, yes, that was my first thought as well, remember? He stops at the study window.

"Ugh, they closed it," he says to Emily. He struggles to open it and groans. "It's locked." Emily joins him and they peek through the dirty panes.

"What if we break the glass?" Michael suggests. "Then we could unlock the window and crawl in."

Emily shakes her head. "That's illegal! Breaking into someone else's house."

"But it's Mr. Starek's sister's house," Michael counters. "He told us we could go inside."

Impatient with this discussion, I fly between them again, almost brushing Emily's nose.

"Mirabelle," she gasps. "Stop that. You're too close."

I loop-the-loop through the air to get their full attention, and then glide around back to the screened porch.

It takes them a few minutes to figure out where I went, but soon they turn the corner. I am waiting, perched on the handle of the porch door.

"What is it, Mirabelle? What do you want?" Emily asks.

Michael runs up to me and tugs the handle. Of course the door won't open, with the hook secured inside. But when I flutter up to the hole in the screen, he knows exactly what to do.

"Look," he says to Emily. "I can reach my hand in and unhook it. We can get in."

Emily joins him, her mouth pursed skeptically. "Maybe you can get into the porch," she says. "But there are locks on the house door."

Her protests don't matter. Michael has already pushed his hand through the hole that Sebastian, Oliver, and I made in the screen. He fumbles for a minute, then lifts the metal hook out of its ring.

The door creaks as he opens it, and we all enter the porch, even me. I have to make sure they find the way inside.

I needn't have worried. Michael immediately drops to his knees by the pet door, lifting the flap.

"You're going through that?" Emily wrinkles her nose. "There's no way I can fit."

"It's okay," he tells her. "I'll get inside and open up the study window. You can crawl in that way."

"Michael..." she starts to protest, but he lifts the rubber flap of the pet door and sticks his head inside the house.

For a minute, I'm worried. Michael is small, but even so, his shoulders look too wide to squeeze through the narrow metal frame of the opening. He pulls his head back out and I'm afraid he's giving up. But then he puts one arm through, followed by his head, and then his shoulders, twisted. The other arm is pressed against his body.

Emily and I watch him wriggle his torso and skinny hips over the rim of the pet door until only his legs are left on our side, flailing helplessly in the air. With a grunt, he squirms all the way through.

"I'm in!" he calls, triumphant.

"Wow." Emily is impressed. "I didn't think you would fit. Okay, I'll meet you at the study window."

She turns and pushes the porch door open, beckoning to me. "Come on, Mirabelle. You don't want to get trapped in here."

Does Emily really think I am foolish enough to get myself imprisoned inside this porch? She must not realize I can fly through the hole in the screen. For heaven's sake, I *made* the hole in the screen.

But I decide to let Emily imagine that she is rescuing me. I know this about humans, despite the ones who hunt animals, the ones who are afraid of us, and the ones who are cruel to us: humans love to believe they've helped a wild creature in distress. It makes them feel merciful, and powerful.

I fly out into the yard, and then swoop to the rhododendron bush beside the study window. I can see Michael's face through the streaked glass, his forehead creased in concentration as he tries to push the window open. "I unlocked it," he says, his words muffled. "But the window is stuck."

"I'll bang on it," Emily offers. She strikes the upper window a few times with her palm, making a loud, sharp noise that would scare me away if I didn't know what she was doing.

"Now try it," she orders.

Michael leans his whole weight against the bottom window, shoving it, and it squeaks open an inch. "Great!" Emily says. "Keep pushing."

He keeps at it, and with another bang or two from Emily, the window is open.

"Okay, here goes," Emily says, throwing her arms over the windowsill and heaving her body through the opening. She wriggles, shoves, and pulls her way in, finally scrambling upright.

I fly inside after her, landing on the edge of the piano. I haven't been this close to it since the day I first found it. I stare at its red-gold luster, the dappled, watery pattern in the wood.

Michael laughs with delight. "She's inside with us! But be careful, Mirabelle. Don't scratch it."

Of course I'll be careful! I would never scratch a historical instrument like this. That makes me a little mad, so I hop over to the brass arm of a lamp and watch from there.

Emily helps Michael raise the lid, and we all stare at the Pleyel, this gorgeous relic from the time of Chopin. I imagine the thousands of fingers that must have touched this wood and these keys over the last two centuries.

"Do you really think Chopin might have played it?" Michael says, his words barely more than a whisper.

"Oh, I want to think so!" Emily's voice is soft, too. "But what are the chances?"

Michael looks at me. "Can I warm up?" he asks Emily.

"Sure," she says. "I'll turn on a light." And then, understanding him, "Oh, you want me to leave you alone. Okay, but don't take too long."

She twists the knob on the lamp and then slips into the hall, closing the door.

Michael and I are alone with the Pleyel.

"Which one?" he whispers to me, sifting through the sheet music on the rack. "Ballade number four? I still don't quite have it right."

He walks to the door and listens for a minute. But I can hear Emily rustling in a distant room, so I know she's not eavesdropping.

Michael sits on the bench and lifts the cover off the keys. This will be the first time he's played the Pleyel since we found out its age. There must be a bit of magic in that, I think—in knowing the long line of pianists who have sat exactly where he's sitting and created beautiful music, through two centuries. Have the people who played it left their mark? Can a piano hold their memories? Does it have a soul?

"Ready?" he asks me.

I am always ready. I hop to the windowsill, where the warm air wafts over me. Michael's long fingers curl gracefully over the keys, and the first plaintive notes of the last ballade pierce the air. I watch his body tense and sway, his dark hair falling over his forehead, his face rapt.

I draw a deep breath and wait through the long, mournful passage until the music thickens lushly. Then I sing.

The clear, ringing notes of my song entwine with each plink of the keys, blending together in a glorious crescendo.

Somehow, finally, we are going to get it right.

We find the B-flat center of the first theme and then slide into the second section, which is technically the most challenging part of the entire piece. And then we are in the climax, in D-flat, soaring high without the slightest heaviness or roughness in the tone.

I feel like I am flying up, up, up, climbing through the sky to the top of a great peak.

When we finish and the last notes fade from the air, Michael turns to me, his cheeks flushed. "That's it," he says.

And I barely have time to hop through the window back to the shrubbery before the door swings open and Emily cries, "Michael! You did it!"

29

A Perfect Match

So that is how we spend the afternoon: Michael at the piano, Emily next to him, me just outside the open window but still with my friends. Michael practices for a long time. Now that he's figured out the last ballade—now that the Pleyel has revealed the piece's meaning to him—he plays it again and again. It flows through his fingers like water.

"Michael," Emily murmurs as he plays. "It's perfect."

He plays and plays, the music washing over us, both thrilling and inevitable.

When he finishes, Emily's eyes are sparkling with excitement. "If you play it that well at the competition...oh, Michael, how can you not win?"

Michael beams at her. "It feels different. It feels like I finally found a way *inside* the music."

"You did!" Emily says. "I can't wait for Mr. Starek to hear this. But it's late. I should take you home."

No, stop! The painting! I want to show them the painting.

I swoop inside, flying in agitated circles over the piano.

Emily jerks back in surprise. "Sheesh, Mirabelle, what's the matter now?"

Before the words are out of her mouth, I zoom into the hallway.

I can hear Michael saying, "We'd better follow her. Otherwise she'll get shut up inside the house."

Honestly! I have no idea why these two think I have so little sense that I would get myself trapped in Halina's house—especially when I was the one who showed them the way in. But I'm on a mission, so I don't have time to be annoyed. I fly to the wooden post of the banister, waiting for them.

"Mirabelle," Emily says. "Don't you understand? It's time to go."

As soon as they're both close to me, I fly up the stairs and, once again, wait on the railing, where they can see me.

Emily frowns. "What's up there?"

"I don't know. I never went upstairs. Did you? Can we check it out?" Michael starts up the staircase, but Emily intervenes.

"I don't know, Michael. This house is so full of stuff— I'm just worried something will fall on you. Or the floor will collapse! I don't think we should go poking around."

Is she kidding me? Poking around is exactly the thing we should be doing! That's how I found the painting of the piano.

I fly a few feet down the stairs toward Michael, then zip back up to the top railing. I feel like a hummingbird, with all my flitting and hovering. Goldfinches weren't designed to fly this way, let me tell you. It's very tiring.

"She wants me to follow her," Michael says. "I'll be quick."

He climbs the stairs lickety-split, with Emily protesting from below, and picks his way past piles of books and overflowing boxes, following me into the bedroom. I flutter through the gloom into the shaft of afternoon sunlight, and then to the spot where the painting of the piano leans against the wall.

I land right on its ornate golden frame.

"Huh," Michael says, coming closer.

And then: "Hey…"

And then, urgently: "EMILY!"

He is crouched next to the painting when she hurries into the room. "What's the matter?" she asks.

"Look what Mirabelle found," he says. "It's a picture of the Pleyel! *Our* Pleyel."

Emily comes and kneels beside him. "Are you sure?"

Her face leans so close I could almost hop onto her nose. I can see the little wisps of brown hair that curl near her ears, the sheen of sweat on her neck.

"Wow," she breathes. "It does look like the piano. It has that same wavy pattern in the wood…and the little brass flowers along the side.…" She hesitates, frowning. "But we'd have to compare them to be sure. Why would someone paint a picture of just the piano…? It's weird, right? I mean, you can't even see the keys."

"Yeah," Michael agrees. "But the colors are cool. Let's carry it downstairs so we can see them side by side."

Emily stands up. "I don't know, Michael. It's pretty big. Do you think we can lift it?"

"Sure," Michael says. "I'm strong."

Emily looks torn, chewing her bottom lip. "Okay, let's try. Let me take this end and I'll walk backward down the stairs. Just be sure you don't trip. It looks old—we should be careful we don't bang it against anything."

They squat on either side of the canvas, and I discreetly fly into the hallway. If they *do* drop it, I don't want to be anywhere nearby. They grunt and heave it into the air, and then come staggering onto the landing, with Emily negotiating her way backward down the stairs.

"Easy," she tells Michael. "Be careful of the railing."

"I am," he says. "It's not even that heavy."

"Well, not for you," Emily says, panting, as she steps backward one stair at a time. "I've got all the weight on me."

Finally, they've got it downstairs. They negotiate their way through the forest of Halina's things into the study. Gently, they lower the painting to the floor and lean it against the piano.

Emily turns on another light, flooding the room, and immediately I can see that for all its darkness, the painting glows with color. There are reds and golds swirling through the brown of the piano, creating patterns and textures and infusing it with light. The vase of flowers sparkles with jewel-like radiance.

Emily squints at it, looking back and forth between the painting and the Pleyel.

"It's the same," Michael declares. "Can't you see? It has the swirl here, and here, and it has that whoosh of gold that looks like a wave curling back on itself." And the lily pad, I want to say. The patterns are identical.

Emily is nodding slowly. "Yeah. But why would somebody paint the piano? It's almost like a portrait, but it doesn't even show the keyboard."

"Maybe because it's so old?" Michael suggests.

Emily's brow creases. "I wonder who made it. You don't see a name anywhere, do you? Let's check."

They are just tilting the painting to inspect it more closely when Emily's cell phone rings, shattering the quiet.

"It's your mom," she says to Michael, and then, "Hi, Mrs. Jin. Yes, we're coming right now. Sorry! We lost track of time, practicing. Yes, it's going really well." She smiles at Michael. "*Really* well. He'll be home soon."

And then it's a mad scramble to leave. "You crawl out the window first and then I'll close up," Emily says. "We need to put everything back the way we found it. Except for this window—I'll leave it cracked open so it's easier for us to get back in."

"What about the painting?" Michael asks. "Do we have to put it back upstairs?"

"Ugh, it's too heavy, and we don't have time," Emily says. She glances around quickly. "Let's slide it behind that chair," she says, "with those other pictures. There's so much stuff down here, I don't think anyone from the bank would notice one more thing."

Together, they carry the painting to the corner of the room and place it behind the large wing chair. Then they close the piano lid.

Michael climbs through the open window, and I fly after him into the late afternoon sun.

We watch together as Emily shuts off the lights, clambers through the window herself, and closes the screen and the window almost all the way, leaving just a crack open.

Minutes later, we are together in the yard. Emily and Michael hurry toward the sedan.

"See you later, Mirabelle," Michael calls to me.

"Fly safe," Emily says.

And as I flap up into the sky to head for home, I think how nice it is to have friends who want to see me later, and who care that I fly safe.

30

The Final Push

The competition is now only days away! We have been sneaking back to Halina's house every chance we get, for Michael to practice on the Pleyel. At first, none of us knew how we would manage this. Life is suddenly very complicated. Michael is at school during the day, so he can only practice in the afternoons and on weekends (though I can tell that the practicing is taking his mind off the new school, because right now, there is only room in his head for Chopin). He was supposed to be going to Mr. Starek's house for his final lessons, but Mr. Starek has been so sick, he can't teach. The old man keeps telling everyone not to worry, that this cough is just the same one he has gotten before, that he will be better in no time...but we are all worried, even so. Mrs. Jin drops off a canister of special soup that she leaves on his porch, and Emily is always calling to check on him and see if she can bring him food or medicine.

"No, no," he tells them, "it isn't necessary. I am doing fine. I just need to rest."

The competition is so soon, and Michael is so close to being ready, that Mrs. Jin has decided Emily should take over the teaching for these last few days. Now, of course, Mrs. Jin assumes Michael is practicing at Emily's house, but because Emily has been picking him up from school and driving him home, his mother has no clue. In fact, each day at the time of the lesson, we go straight to Halina's, straight to the Pleyel.

I worry about this, because it almost feels like a lie. But Michael keeps saying it's a secret. "We have to keep it secret," he and Emily say to each other. So I keep it secret, too. I don't even tell Mother that I've been going to Halina's house every day with Michael to practice.

Sometimes I wonder, though: What's the difference between a secret and a lie? A secret probably feels like a lie to someone who loves you.

Ever since the storm, Mother has been less keen on me being out of the neighborhood. I know she wouldn't like it one bit that I'm flying all the way to Halina's house so often. Of course, she's busy with the little sisters—or the little monsters, as Sebastian calls them—who are almost ready to fly. You're surprised, right?

They were just born, you're thinking. But we birds mature quickly, unlike humans. A baby goldfinch will start testing its wings and trying to fly when it's just a couple of weeks old. At that stage, it's called a fledgling.

They are starting to have personalities, those babies. They are still loud and demanding, that's for sure, always chirping for food. But Serena has already tried to flit around a little, and Lina and George have become good friends, smoothing each other's feathers. They are excited to see us whenever Sebastian, Oliver, and I come to the nest, because we often bring food for them.

Mother is so concerned about them falling out of the nest before they can fly that she is keeping an extra-close eye on them. Have you ever found a baby bird on the ground? Here's something humans believe about baby birds that isn't true: people think if they touch a baby bird, the mother will abandon it because it smells like humans. Well, that's a bunch of malarkey. We birds don't recognize each other by smell. We don't even have such a great sense of smell. Seeing and hearing—that's what we do best, certainly better than humans.

Still, you don't usually need to rescue baby birds. If you see a baby bird with feathers that's hopping or flitting around, it will be fine on its own. The mother bird is watching over it, and will keep feeding it and checking on it as its wings get stronger and it learns how to fly. Just please protect it from cats and dogs.

On the other hand, if you see a tiny, alien-looking bird with wrinkled skin and not many feathers, that is a nestling, and it needs to go back in its nest. So, look for a nest above the spot where you found the baby bird, and if you can, very gently, try to put it back inside.

But otherwise, don't touch birds! We don't like it.

Anyway, Mother hasn't wanted Sebastian, Oliver, and me to leave the yard since the storm. But I told her that Mr. Starek's cough has come back and I think she assumes I'm hanging around his bedroom window to cheer him up, the way I did last spring. And that's true—I *have* been checking on him. But there's no time to sit by his window, because Michael and I have so much work to do! We are busy practicing the last ballade to make sure it sounds just the way Chopin would have wanted it to.

And Michael has also been practicing what Mr. Starek told him to, how to play without a care in the world, even when he's feeling nervous. As soon as we get to Halina's, he races around the backyard and does jumping jacks, until he's red in the face and panting, his cheeks shining with sweat. Then he and Emily quickly climb through the window, she leaves the room, and Michael sits down at the piano and dives right into the Minute Waltz. His fingers fly over the keys and I joyfully sing along.

It really does sound different when he plays this way, so loose and free. It's almost like he's making up the music on the spot, even though, of course, it's a two-hundred-year-old melody written with precision by Chopin.

One day after our warm-up, Michael turns to me and whispers urgently, "You're coming with me, right, Mirabelle? To Hartford? You have to!"

Come to the festival? There's been no time to make a plan, with all our hard work, but I never dreamed of not going with Michael. I have to be with him when he plays.

Michael continues, "I won't be able to play like this in the competition if you're not there. That time you missed the lesson was a *disaster*."

I bow my head with shame. I still feel badly about that, leaving Michael on his own the day of the storm.

Of course I will go to the festival! It's our destiny—I'm sure of it.

"You'll come, right? I need you."

He holds out his finger, and I fly to the tip, gripping the thin bone.

Yes, yes, I will, I will! I can just imagine myself in front of all those people, in a real concert hall, with all the other musicians.

Michael's face is so close to me, his eyes so intense. "I have to win, Mirabelle. I just have to. If I win, I'll get the money! Ten thousand dollars." He hesitates, his forehead creasing. "And then maybe I can help Mr. Starek keep Halina's house...and the piano."

I stare at him in surprise. So that's what he's thinking—that the prize money could save the Pleyel! Oh, wouldn't that be wonderful?

But would ten thousand dollars be enough? I have no idea.

It is nice that Michael is thinking of Mr. Starek, though. The old man has been resting so that he'll recover in time for the festival, but he still seems so sick. It worries me.

Michael's gaze is anxious. I look up at him, cocking my head.

"We'd have to figure out how to bring you, in a safe way." He bites his lip. "I'll be taking my backpack." He bends over and shows it to me, pulling at the fabric. "Look, these little nets on the side are for water bottles. I could put you in one of them, really gently."

I don't like the sound of that. It would remind me too much of being caught in a net. And anybody could see me.

Michael thinks for a minute. "I know! I'll put a cup in there, and you can sit inside it, so nobody will notice you. What do you think?"

That sounds like a better idea. I'm so excited, I flutter right up to Michael's shoulder and land there.

He throws back his head and laughs. "Does that mean you'll do it?"

Emily opens the door, and I fly quickly back to the windowsill.

"What are you laughing about?" she asks. "You're supposed to be warming up!"

"I am," Michael says. "I'm just laughing at Mirabelle. At something she did."

We look at each other, and then I hop back to the branch of the rhododendron.

"Are you ready?" Emily asks.

Michael nods, and he begins to play, right through the entire repertoire: the prelude, the étude, and finally the last ballade.

The whole time, as I listen to the notes cascade over each other, lush and gorgeous, I think: I'm going to the festival! With Michael! And all the other musicians. Because that's where I belong. I am, after all, a musical star.

31

Ready or Not

Finally, it's Friday, the day that Michael is leaving for the competition in Hartford. I can scarcely believe it. The Chopin Festival is tomorrow—the thing we have been waiting for, and working for, since the beginning of summer. After taking so long to get here, everything is happening at once. The plan is for Mrs. Jin, Mr. Starek, Emily, and Michael to drive down together today and spend the night at a hotel. Michael has found a cup that will fit in the netted side of his backpack, and at the last two lessons, during our warm-up, we have practiced having me hide in there. To tell you the truth, it makes me very nervous squeezing into such a confined space. But I trust Michael.

I have not told Mother about my plan because she would

never in a million years allow it. But this morning, I secretly tell Sebastian and Oliver that I am going with Michael to the festival. I don't want my family to worry when I don't come home at night.

"You're going in a *car*?" Sebastian says. "Why not fly?"

"You're going to stay *overnight*?" Oliver marvels. "That sounds risky."

"Michael needs me," I tell them. "And it will all be fine. But please don't say anything to Mother! You know how she worries."

"She's going to worry when you're not in the roost tonight," Sebastian says.

"Can't you do a sleepover with the cousins?" I ask. "In the Garcias' maple tree? Then you can tell her I'm waiting for you there."

"We can try," Ollie says. "But she may get suspicious. When are you coming home?"

"Tomorrow," I promise. "Definitely tomorrow, after the competition."

With that plan in place, I fly to the yew bush by Mr. Starek's door to wait for Michael. I can't help fretting about the old man. He has not gotten better as fast as we all hoped. I have barely seen him—he hasn't refilled the bird feeder in days, and he doesn't come into the garden, even though the weather is warm.

Whenever I fly up to check on him, I don't bother to hide in the tree branches. I land right on the windowsill. I can see the frail mound of his body under the sheets, resting, waiting to get stronger. I try to cheer myself up. I heard him on the phone with Mrs. Jin and Michael just yesterday, and he said he was coming. He said he wouldn't miss it for the world.

I'm perched in the shrubbery when Mrs. Jin's car pulls into the driveway. Michael jumps out with his backpack over one shoulder and runs to the front door to get Mr. Starek (and, of course, *me*, but nobody knows that). He looks for me immediately, and grins when he sees me. "Hey!" he whispers. "Ready?"

Mrs. Jin puts down her window, calling to Michael to hurry.

Michael clangs the bell, once, twice, three times.

We both listen at the door, but there is only hushed silence inside the house.

Michael turns back to his mother, uncertain.

Emily calls from the front seat, "Should I try the phone?"

"I'll knock," Michael yells. He bangs loudly on the big wooden door.

But nobody comes.

I realize with a strange, sinking feeling that Mr. Starek must be too sick to answer it.

Michael waits on the porch, shifting from one foot to the other. Although the September day is full of noises—lawn mowers and car engines and distant shouts from someone's backyard—no sound at all comes from the house.

I hop to the end of a branch and look down at Michael.

"Can you check on him?" Michael asks.

That's just what I intend to do. Quickly, I fly around the corner of the house and up to Mr. Starek's bedroom, peering through the window. It is cracked open, and I can see him clearly. He is lying on his side in bed, his face a wince of pain.

I have never seen him look like this. Not even in the spring when he was sick.

Suddenly, I feel afraid.

He coughs, barely able to catch his breath. His eyes never open.

Michael is standing on the lawn below me, calling softly, "Mirabelle!"

I don't know what to do. A cold blade of dread slices through me.

I flutter down to Michael, and we head back to the front yard.

Mrs. Jin is at the front door now, beckoning. "Michael, if we don't leave now, we'll be late for registration. Mr. Starek must be resting. I know he wants to come, but I told you yesterday when I spoke to him that he didn't sound up to the trip."

"But he said he would be there," Michael cries. "He has to see me play."

"He has to get better," Mrs. Jin says firmly. "It's important for him to take care of himself."

"Can't we talk to him?"

Mrs. Jin frowns with exasperation. "Why don't you try the phone? Maybe he can speak with you quickly."

I clutch a branch overhead as Michael takes his cell phone from his backpack, tapping the number. Amazingly, Mr. Starek answers. I hear the low rumble of his voice through the phone. I can tell from Michael's responses that the old man is wishing him luck, giving his blessing, urging him on. Oh, why doesn't he tell Michael how sick he is?

"I will," Michael says. "I know. I will. I just wish—"

There's a pause, and then Michael says, "Are you sure you're okay? You don't sound so good."

Mrs. Jin tilts her head, her eyes flashing concern. "Let me talk to him, Michael," she says, taking the phone.

Thank goodness. Now they will know.

She murmurs into it briefly, asking questions and nodding. "All right, all right, as long as your doctor says so. We'll come straight here after the festival so we can tell you what happened. Yes, we're about to leave—I know, there could be traffic. Here's Michael."

Michael takes back the phone and says, "Okay. I will. I'll call you as soon as it's over. I hope you feel better! Bye."

Mrs. Jin walks briskly back to the car. I can't stand it. Are they really going to leave him?

They don't know how sick he is.

If they knew, they wouldn't go.

Even for this thing that has been the work of the entire summer. Even for this chance for Michael to play Chopin and win the competition, win the prize money, win the scholarships.

Even for this chance for me to be a musical star.

"Coming," Michael shouts to his mother. "Just one thing." He's holding his backpack by the strap and he swings it up through the air, showing me the blue plastic cup wedged into the netted pouch on the side. I flutter down to a lower branch.

He comes so close to me, and his face is huge, his hand outstretched.

"Ready, Mirabelle?"

I look at the little shelter that he's made for me, just so I can go with him. It feels like a promise between us.

"What's the matter?" he asks.

I think about Mr. Starek in his bedroom, sick and alone.

"Michael!" his mother calls. "We have to leave *now*!"

Even though it nearly kills me, I fly up to the top of the bell, the bell where I landed so many weeks ago to teach him my name. I sit there, out of his reach.

His dark eyes are desperate. "Mirabelle, what are you doing? You're coming with me, right?"

I would do anything for him! You know that, don't you? Every cell in my body wants to swoop down into his open palm, go with him, be there when he plays.

"Please, Mirabelle," he begs. "Please! You have to come. I can't do it without you."

Oh, how can I explain what I feel for Michael? It is a mashed-up sense of belonging…like he is *my* boy, but I belong to him…and I am *his* bird, but he belongs to me.

And now I think that George Sand knew what she was talking

about when she said, "There is only one happiness in this life, to love and be loved."

But...the old man.

How can I leave him?

"MICHAEL!" Mrs. Jin yells.

I stay where I am.

I watch Michael turn, the light catching his glossy hair, black as a raven's wing. Head down, he hurries to the car.

Michael. The old man.

I love them both.

The car pulls away.

32

Help!

I know what you're thinking. How could I not go with Michael? He needs me! It was a pact between us, the certainty that I would be with him when he played. What if he can't do it without me? If he doesn't win, it will be my fault.

Oh, don't make me feel worse.

I used to play a game with myself, thinking about Michael and the old man. Who matters more? For instance, if the old man and the boy were both drowning in a lake, which one would I save?

Okay, forget the fact that goldfinches don't swim. Or that I'm very small and probably couldn't actually save anyone. If I had to choose, who would I save?

The boy, the boy, you say. That's just because he's the one who's most like you. And you're thinking, he has his whole life ahead of him, while the old man has already lived his.

But maybe the long, full weight of the old man's life should count for more. The old man knows so much. And it would all be lost if he died.

I used to play that game. Now I know that none of this is important, this weighing and sorting, trying to figure out who matters more. The truth is, if they were both drowning in a lake, I would choose with my heart.

And my heart would be divided, because I love them both.

As soon as Michael is gone, I fly around the corner of the house to the upstairs bedroom window. I land on the sill, close to the screen.

The room is dark and smells of sickness. The old man lies under the covers, barely moving. His eyes are closed.

I think about his sister dying, and her house full of treasures, and the bank taking all of it, and now the old man so sick that he can't go to the Chopin Festival to see Michael play. He's worked so hard! He's given so much.

It is all so sad and awful I can't stand it.

So when Mr. Starek rolls over in the bed, turned toward the window, his eyes still closed, coughing that dry, scraping cough, I try to make things better.

I draw in a breath, open my beak, and sing for him, the way I did when he was sick last spring.

When I stop, I look at the old man's face, and I have the aching feeling that I may be seeing it for the last time. It is so worn by life, crossed with lines. Delicate blue-green veins ripple the papery surface of his skin; his silver hair is damp and flat.

His eyes flicker open and rest precisely on me. Something seems to pass between us, some kind of impossible understanding.

Oh, I don't want him to die.

He begins to cough again, the wracking, body-shaking cough, and I know I have to help him.

Desperate, I lift off from the branch and fly over the garden, which looks so much the way it always does, green and sparkling in the sunshine. Bees tumble in the flowers, a dragonfly darts through the air. How can this shimmering world not know the old man is dying? How can everything be just as it was?

Then I see Harmony.

She is on the back patio, pacing around and mewing in her annoying way, and it occurs to me that she hasn't been fed. Now, let me tell you, that old cat could stand to lose a few pounds, but seeing her in such a state gives me an idea.

I flutter down to the stone wall of the patio in a haphazard way, rocking unevenly, dropping close to the ground. I'm pretending to be injured, and boy does that get her attention.

She freezes, her pale eyes fixed on me. Her body drops into a crouch, but just as she's about to spring, I flutter a few feet away, as if I am barely able to escape her. This time she slinks toward me, her round belly skimming the flagstones.

Quickly, I fly to the top of the fence that separates Mr. Starek's yard from the Garcia family's. On rare occasions, Harmony has gotten herself over this fence, by jumping from patio wall to barbecue grill to fence post, always in pursuit of something. But once she's in the Garcias' yard, she's stuck. There's not an easy way for her to climb back over. I just have to hope she's hungry enough, and bloodthirsty enough, to follow me.

It's a risky game, of course. But I don't even care about that, because I have to help the old man. Which means I need humans, his neighbors.

I hop unsteadily along the top of the fence, with my wing dragging. I'm quite a good actress, if I do say so myself. I must really look like I'm in bad shape, because I can see the drool glistening on the edge of Harmony's awful mouth.

She hops swiftly onto the patio wall, then in a motion so fast it takes me by surprise, she springs onto the barbecue grill and then launches herself through the air right at me.

Yikes!

I quickly tumble over the fence into the Garcias' yard, and Harmony—after catching her fat belly on the top of the fence in a brief moment of unsteady balancing—comes catapulting after me.

As she races and pounces inches behind me, and I flutter in my broken, pitiful way around the Garcias' back deck, I am beginning to realize all the problems with my plan. What if the Garcias don't notice me? What if they're not even home? I need someone to take Harmony back to Mr. Starek's house and see how sick he is.

Fortunately, one of the Garcia children, the littlest girl, Paula, is standing at the window. She screams.

This is even more drama than I had hoped for.

"Mama! That gray cat is in the yard! And it's trying to catch a bird, a pretty yellow bird."

Why, thank you, Paula.

"Ooooh, look, the bird is sick! The cat is trying to eat it! Mama, come quick."

Mrs. Garcia, God bless her, is there in a flash. She comes out on the deck with a broom and puts it right in Harmony's face, while I pretend to barely have the strength to hop up to the safety of the umbrella table.

Harmony recoils, and Mrs. Garcia drops the broom and scoops her up.

"Oh, Harmony!" she says in reproof. "Were you going to make a nice snack of that poor little goldfinch?"

She steps into the house and slides the screen shut, saying, "Paula, put the broom away. I'll take her back to Mr. Starek's."

Hooray! This is the first step. Someone is going to Mr. Starek's house.

"I'm going to get that hurt bird," Paula announces, "and put it in a box."

What?! Out of the frying pan, into the fire.

"Oh, honey, I would leave it alone," her mother says. "If it's hurt or sick, there's probably nothing we can do for it."

"Maybe it's a baby," Paula protests. "I'm going to make a little house for it and feed it until it gets better."

"Well, don't touch it with your bare hands," her mother warns. "Birds are full of germs."

Excuse me? Thanks a lot, lady.

Uh-oh, here comes Paula with a shoebox.

Since I'm not sick or hurt, it is pretty easy to fly away from her, though I can hear her cries of frustration as I flap over the wall and up to Mr. Starek's roof.

"Wait, Mama!" Paula yells. "The bird flew away. I'm coming with you."

I watch Mrs. Garcia walk up Mr. Starek's driveway, with Harmony squirming in her arms, and Paula trotting after her.

I perch high on the metal rim of the gutter, where nobody can see me. I don't want to cause any more commotion than I already have.

Mrs. Garcia knocks on the door, a few brisk, sharp knocks.

"Now, stop, Harmony," she says, enfolding the cat more securely in her arms. "You'll be back inside in just a minute."

When nobody answers, Mrs. Garcia clangs the bell. It makes a loud, echoing noise.

"Hmmm, maybe he's not home," she says, puzzled.

"What will we do if he's gone?" Paula asks. "Will we keep the cat at our house?"

Uh-oh, I hadn't thought of that.

But Mrs. Garcia isn't deterred. "Let's see if the car's in the garage."

Good thinking! She walks over to the windows of the garage door and peers inside.

"His car's there," she says. "Paula, ring the bell again."

Paula is barely tall enough to reach the string of the bell, but she pulls on it vigorously, too many times.

Clang! Clang! Clang!

"That's enough," her mother says. "Well, maybe he went for a walk. Lucky for Harmony we have a spare key. Run back to the house and get it, will you, Paula? It's in the kitchen desk drawer, on a black-and-white key chain. You'll see it."

I can tell that Paula doesn't much like this idea, but she stomps over the grass back to her own house.

Mrs. Garcia, meanwhile, is looking around Mr. Starek's house with a bit of suspicion. She sees the newspaper in the driveway and picks it up, still holding the struggling Harmony. She hesitates, then walks to the end of the driveway and checks the mailbox. I see her pulling out a stack of mail.

Poor Mr. Starek! Has he been too sick to go to his own mailbox?

Now her arms are full of cat, newspaper, and mail.

"Paula!" she calls. "What's taking so long?"

Finally, Paula appears. "There were a LOT of keys in there," she shouts. "But I found it!"

She dangles the key in front of her and comes running across the yard to her mother. The keychain *is* black and white, like a piano keyboard.

"Okay, can you hold the cat while I open the door?"

"Yes!" Paula says eagerly. She grabs Harmony and smashes the cat against her chest. Harmony mews desperately.

"Don't let her scratch you," her mother warns, fitting the key in the lock.

"Mr. Starek? Mr. Starek, are you here?" she calls, opening the door.

And then they are inside the house, slamming the door behind them.

Now, of course, I can't see or hear anything. What if they just drop off Harmony and go home?

I am so worried about this that I fly back to the tree by Mr. Starek's window. His face is turned away, so I can't see it, and his body is a long, still lump under the sheets.

The door to his bedroom is partly ajar, but I don't notice any movement in the hallway. Maybe they've already left.

Just as my heart is filling with despair, I do see movement. Old Harmony slips through the gap in the door and leaps onto his bed, mewing. She bats his face with one of her paws.

He doesn't move. My heart sinks.

But then I see Mrs. Garcia's face at the bedroom door. "Mr. Starek?" she asks softly.

She hesitates. "Paula, stay there," she calls.

Mrs. Garcia comes into the room and bends over him, gently shaking his shoulder. "Mr. Starek, are you all right?"

I see her lay the back of her hand against his forehead.

Then she straightens sharply. "Paula, find the telephone," she says. "We need to call nine-one-one."

Oh, what a frenzy of activity comes next! Mrs. Garcia speaking urgently into the phone, rushing downstairs, and then, within minutes, the quiet September day is shattered by the sound of sirens.

An ambulance races up to the house, red lights flashing.

It is such a commotion that I am not at all surprised to see Sebastian and Oliver gliding over the garden, looking for me.

"Here," I call to them. "By the window."

"Why are you still here?" Sebastian demands. "I thought you were going to the festival with Michael. What's the emergency?"

I tell them about Mr. Starek being too sick, and me worrying about him and leading Harmony over the fence into the Garcias' yard so that the neighbors would come check on him.

"That was smart," Sebastian admits. "And it worked. But what's wrong with the old man? Is he dead?"

My heart seizes. He can't be dead. He just can't be.

We are all staring through the bedroom window, where there are so many people around the old man's bed, in such a tumult, that they are completely blocking our view.

"I don't know," I answer, feeling hopeless. "Do they call an ambulance if you're dead?"

"They have to call somebody," Sebastian says.

"I can't see a thing," Oliver complains. "Let's go to the front and watch the ambulance."

Which is what we do. Very soon, two people in blue uniforms come out of the house with Mr. Starek on a stretcher between them. A third one is hurrying behind them. The old man's body is covered by a sheet, but I can see his face, pale and slack.

They slide him expertly into the back of the ambulance, and then they all jump inside and the ambulance speeds away, siren blaring.

Mrs. Garcia and Paula stand on the front porch, watching it go.

Is Mr. Starek alive? Is he dead?

Please say something.

"What are they going to do to him?" Paula asks.

"They're taking him to the hospital," Mrs. Garcia answers. "Poor thing."

Paula looks at her mother with wide eyes. "Is he going to die?"

I feel a beat of hope. He's alive! At least right now, the old man is alive.

"I don't know," her mother says. "He's very sick. It's lucky we came over here this morning, Paula…all because you saw his cat."

"It's all because of me," Paula agrees, clearly pleased with herself.

But I am so relieved, I don't even mind.

33

Waiting

The hospital is in the next town over, but that doesn't keep me from wanting to check on the old man as soon as possible. I don't expect Mother to allow it, but when she hears how sick he is, she wants to visit him herself.

"Oh, I do hope he gets better," she says. "The poor man. Hospitals are so big—it will be hard to find his room. But I will have a look around and see if it's safe for you to go, Mirabelle." She turns to the boys. "Sebastian! Oliver! I need you to help Mirabelle. You three watch the babies while I'm gone."

The babies sense that something's up and start a chorus of protest. Mother chirps at them soothingly. "I'll be back," she says, and then reminds us, "They'll need to be fed soon."

This is nothing new. They always need to be fed.

As Mother flies away, she calls over one wing, "Don't let any of them try to follow me. They're not ready yet."

As soon as she leaves, the babies make a racket like nobody's business, cheeping and wailing. Sebastian, Ollie, and I are poor substitutes for Mother and they know it.

"Mother! Mother! Mother! Mother! Mother! Mother! Mother!" they cry.

"Oh, settle down," Sebastian snaps. "She's coming back soon."

George tries to hurl herself over the edge of the nest, and Lina is ready to follow. Ollie and I have to beat our wings at their heads to stop them.

"Ugh," he groans. "Let's just feed them. That's the only thing that ever shuts them up."

So we spend the afternoon dropping thistle seeds into their gaping mouths and trying to distract them—which works for short bursts, and then they start clamoring again.

Our ears are ringing by the time Mother finally gets back.

I am filled with dread when I see her. What if she has bad news about the old man? I remember how lifeless his face looked, right before the ambulance took him away.

"Did you find him?" I can barely squeak. "How is he?"

Mother lands on the edge of the nest, looking grim. "I did find him, but I had to circle the whole building twice, peeking in every room. He seems very sick, Mirabelle. Doctors and nurses kept coming in and out, tending to him."

"Is he going to die?" Sebastian asks.

"I don't know," Mother says. "But he is where he needs to be if he has any hope of getting better."

"Can I go to him?" I ask. "Please, Mother?"

"It's too late, today, Mirabelle. He needs his rest. But you can visit tomorrow. He's on the second floor. His room faces the fountain, and there's a big elm next to the window."

Tomorrow! Tomorrow is the day of the festival. Oh, how I wish I were there. As worried as I am about the old man, I can't stop thinking about Michael. Is he ready to perform? Will he be able to play the way he needs to if I'm not with him?

I think of the magic of our duets, the way my singing and his playing seemed to create something entirely new. It was Chopin, but it was more than Chopin.

And now Michael has to play by himself.

Well, Emily's there, of course, and Emily is wonderful. She will boost his confidence—I know that. But it isn't the same as having me. Michael must think I abandoned him! What kind of friend would leave him on his own at the most important moment? Just when he needed me most?

Not to mention that it was *my* chance, too. Everything I've dreamed of, my artistic destiny. Who knows what I might have learned from those other musicians?

Sometimes I feel like I've ruined everything.

But what could I do? I couldn't leave the old man.

Mother likes to say, you must always do right by the one you are with. And in that moment, when Michael was leaving for the Chopin Festival, the one I was with and the one who needed me most was the old man.

Argh, I hope Michael is not angry with me. And I hope he can play better than anyone so that he will WIN.

He wants so badly to get that prize money. Even if it isn't enough to save Halina's house and the piano, it's still a lot. It would help. I know it would.

The very next morning, as the day dawns for the festival, I fly all the way to the big beige block of the hospital building. The first rosy streaks of sunrise are lighting the sky, but the human world is still asleep. The houses are quiet; the streets are empty. Only birds are awake, singing to greet the dawn.

I circle the hospital, looking for a window facing a fountain, with an elm beside it. I find it in no time, thanks to Mother's excellent directions. I land on the rough concrete sill and peer inside.

The old man lies in a high bed with metal railings and wheels. His eyes are closed, and his face looks as pale and withered as it did yesterday. There are tubes coming out of his nose, and tubes coming out of his arm, and next to the bed is a tall contraption that looks like a coatrack, with plastic bags hanging from it.

A woman in a loose blue shirt and matching pants stands at the foot of the bed, checking a chart.

She glances up when I hop along the windowsill.

"Why, hello!" she says, smiling. And then, "Mr. Starek, you have a visitor."

The old man doesn't open his eyes or stir. The white drift of sheets over his chest rises and falls.

When the nurse finally leaves the room, I flutter to the spot where the window is open a few inches.

I think of Michael. Soon he'll be in the concert hall, getting ready to play. The old man isn't there to see his hard work come to fruition, and Michael is probably the last student he will ever teach.

All this makes me so sad I can't stand it.

I picture Michael playing the prelude, "Tree Full of Songs," and an idea takes shape in my mind.

If the old man can't go to the festival, maybe I can bring the festival to him. I can't perform for a room full of strangers—I can't show them my talent and hear their applause—but I can perform Michael's Chopin repertoire right here, for the old man. I know every piece by heart.

I will sing for him. I will sing him up, up, up from the terrible sickness stealing his breath and pinning him to the bed. I will sing him well again.

Is it safe? Well, the rest of the world is still asleep, and the old man is so far gone, if he hears me at all, it will be deep inside himself, in that place of memories and dreams. Where Halina waits for him.

I open my beak and the notes dance through the air, fast and lush and free. Somewhere, miles away, Michael will be playing this prelude soon. And maybe the thread that connects us can stretch over the vast distance and send my singing straight into his ear, down through his blood and his veins to his fingertips, making his fingers *sing*.

I can feel the music swelling inside me, tingling under the surface of my skin. It billows out into the air until the rest of me disappears. I become only song.

The old man's eyelids flicker. His head turns slightly toward me.

I sing and sing, the notes leaping and curling over each other, blending and trilling and dancing.

I finish Chopin's prelude in D major, "Tree Full of Songs." And then, drawing a deep breath, I sing his étude in A minor, "Winter Wind." And when the last mournful notes of that piece subside, my lungs fill with the ballade in F minor, the last ballade, the most beautiful and difficult piece of music ever written.

As I sing it, I am Michael, and the Pleyel, and Chopin sitting in a long-ago salon, playing from his very soul.

When the ballade ends, it takes me a minute to even remember where I am. My whole body is shaking. I open my eyes and look around, and I see that the old man has also opened his eyes.

He is staring right at me, his face full of awe.

Quickly, I come to my senses. I fly away.

34

Return

It is dusk, the light almost gone, and we have all settled in our leafy roosts, when suddenly headlights flood the old man's driveway. I know that it must be Michael returning from the competition. Oh my goodness, what happened?

"Can I go?" I beg Mother. "Please? It's Michael—he's come back!"

Mother does not seem pleased. "It's late, Mirabelle—" she starts to protest, but before she can forbid it, I zip out of the holly tree.

"I'll be quick, I promise," I call to her. "I have to find out if he won!"

By the time I get to the front of the house, Michael, Emily, and

Mrs. Jin are all standing on Mr. Starek's front porch. They've clanged the bell twice. Now they're pounding on the wooden door.

I land in the bushes with a rustle and wait for him to see me.

Michael, Michael, Michael!

He turns immediately, his face flushed, his eyes sparkling even in the dusky light.

"We have to tell him!" Michael says, speaking to his mother, but I know it's meant for me. "We have to tell him I got second place! Against kids so much older than me. I was the youngest person in the youth category."

Second place? *Second* place?

My heart sinks. He wasn't the best.

Is it because I wasn't with him?

I am flooded with guilt. And of course that means no prize money. What are we going to do now?

But Michael seems so happy. It's as if he won not just the youth category, but the trophy for the entire festival.

"AND…" He takes a deep breath, now looking directly at me. "I got the Frédéric Chopin Artistic Interpretation Award. They're sending me to Warsaw to play at the International Chopin Competition!"

What? I can't believe my ears. Michael is going to Poland?! Where Chopin lived and played when he was Michael's age. Oh my heavens, this is a possibility I never even thought of.

Mrs. Jin is smiling so widely, her face so filled with joy, I can see what she must have looked like as a little girl…when she was Michael's age, when she played the piano herself. "It was exquisite, Michael. You deserved all of it."

Emily is grinning, too, but now she steps back to squint up at the windows of the house.

"Is he asleep?" she asks. "It's not that late, but the whole house is dark. Do you think he's all right?"

Mrs. Jin looks worried. "He did seem quite ill."

How can I explain what has happened to Mr. Starek? I am flummoxed by this until I hear a clattering sound next door and see the shadowy figure of Mrs. Garcia pulling her recycling bin back toward the garage. She pauses when she notices the trio on Mr. Starek's front stoop.

"Hi," she calls. "Can I help you?"

"We're here to see Mr. Starek," Mrs. Jin responds. "My son is a piano student of his and we've just come back from a competition."

"He's not home," Mrs. Garcia says. "He's over at Mercy Hospital."

Michael and Emily gasp, and Mrs. Jin says, "Oh, I'm so sorry to hear that! Do you know what's wrong?"

"I called to check on him a little while ago," Mrs. Garcia says. "He has pneumonia." She shakes her head, clucking. "He was so sick yesterday! We had to call an ambulance. But they said he's doing better today, fortunately."

My whole body slumps with relief.

"Thank you for letting us know," Mrs. Jin says as Mrs. Garcia rolls the clunky bin into her garage.

"Mom," Michael says, tugging his mother's sleeve. "Can we go see him? We have to tell him what happened. I could never have played so well without him, and without that Pleyel piano at his sister's house."

He flashes a glance at me and I know what he's thinking without him saying it. He's not mad at me! And he's definitely not mad about second place.

"Please, Mom," he begs.

Emily turns to Mrs. Jin. "If Mr. Starek is feeling better, he will be desperate to know how Michael did. I can drive Michael over to the hospital if you don't have time."

Mrs. Jin hesitates. "Visiting hours are probably over for the day, and I'm sure he needs his rest."

"Mom, I have to see him," Michael says. "Hearing what happened might help him get better."

"And even if we can't see him," Emily adds, "we can at least leave him a note."

"All right," Mrs. Jin decides. "Let me call and see if you can visit briefly."

There is some discussion on the phone with the hospital—is Mr. Starek well enough for visitors? How many? How long can they stay? It turns out that visiting hours are ending at eight o'clock, so there isn't much time. Mrs. Jin says she will wait in the car while Michael and Emily run in quickly to give him the news.

I don't like flying at night, and Mother certainly wouldn't approve, but I want to see the old man again—I want to see his face when they tell him about the festival. As Mrs. Jin and Emily get into the car, Michael lingers behind, standing near the branch where I'm perched.

"Mirabelle," he says. "It's true. I played it just the way I wanted to." He shakes his head, smiling at me. "I was really worried about doing it without you. I didn't think I could. I was so scared."

I hop to the end of the branch and cock my head at him, listening. I need for him to know how much I wished I were there.

His voice drops to a whisper. "But it was like I could hear you. When I started to play, I could hear your song inside my head. So I just played along with your singing, the way I always do."

Our duet! This makes me so happy, I can't help myself. I flutter out of the shrubbery and land right on his head, feeling his thick black hair beneath my feet.

He laughs out loud. "And you know what? I wasn't even thinking about winning. I was just thinking about the music. That was the only thing that mattered."

"Michael!" his mother calls. "What are you doing? We need to get to the hospital by eight."

And before she has a chance to glimpse me in the darkness, I swoop away, up, up, up into the night sky.

Since I've been to the hospital on my own, I know the way. Though autumn is coming, the night air is still warm, and full of little flitting creatures—mosquitoes, flying beetles, gnats. Two things I have to watch out for: bats, which are fluttering thickly around the rooftops, feasting on insects; and owls, which may be hiding in the distant trees, waiting to feast on *me*.

I stay out in the open, away from the groves of trees by the river, and fly over the neighborhoods and roads to Mercy Hospital. The highway streams with lights as cars zoom past below. Which one is Mrs. Jin's? It's too dark to tell.

I get to the hospital before they do, and fly to the old man's window. I can tell immediately that he is feeling better. He is sitting up in bed—it is a funny bed that folds in the middle, so the top half of it can rise up—and he's watching the news on the television that hangs from the wall. He doesn't notice me when I land on the windowsill.

A few minutes later, there is a soft knock on the door, and Michael and Emily come in. Michael runs to his bedside.

Mr. Starek's eyes widen and his face breaks into a smile. "Michael! I've been thinking of you all day. How did it go?"

"I didn't win," Michael blurts out. "I didn't win the prize money." Even from where I sit on the windowsill, I can see his small face, fixed on Mr. Starek's. Does he expect the old man to be disappointed? Mr. Starek didn't even know about Michael's plan to use the prize money to save Halina's piano. I steel myself for regret, just in case.

But the old man is nodding intently, listening.

Michael continues, "I came in second! And I won another prize! It's a new one, a prize for—" He turns to Emily.

"Artistic interpretation," Emily says, completing his sentence.

"For playing the music the way Chopin meant it to be played," Michael says proudly. "I won that one!"

"You did?" Mr. Starek's face, which has been so gray and sad, is beaming. "Well, that is wonderful, Michael! That sounds even better than winning first place! Congratulations! I knew you would do very well."

"He was amazing," Emily says. "He played all the pieces beautifully, especially the last ballade."

"I was really nervous," Michael says. "But I did what you taught me. I played with *abandon*."

Mr. Starek smiles. "You should be so proud of yourself."

"And"—Michael looks ready to burst—"I get to go to Warsaw! To play in the International Chopin Competition next spring!"

"Oh! How marvelous. Poland…" Mr. Starek's voice softens. "How I would love to see that."

"Maybe you'll feel better by then and you can come," Michael says. "You *are* feeling better, aren't you?"

The old man nods. "I am. Much better now, especially after hearing this news." He smiles at Michael and peers out the window, where I am sitting on the concrete sill, behind the dark glass. None of them can see me outside the bright room.

"Do you know something?" he says to Michael. "I had the strangest, most beautiful dream. I dreamed a little goldfinch came to my window and sang your entire festival repertoire…the prelude, the étude, and the ballade. Sang it perfectly. It was like my own private concert."

Michael laughs, leaning on the bed. "Really?" he says. "That's a cool dream." He smiles a small, secret smile.

And my heart swells with happiness, even though not one of them knows I'm watching.

35

Art Among Friends

A week later, Mr. Starek comes home from the hospital. The world seems almost back to normal. The Garcias have been taking care of the awful Harmony at their house, which was a nice reprieve for all of us goldfinches, but now she's back to her old tricks, crouching in the bushes near the bird feeder and waiting for the least misstep when we go there for a snack.

Do you want to know how the babies are doing? They are ready to fly! They keep taking little, short hopping flights around the nest, coming back to be fed. Soon they will be flying as easily as Oliver, Sebastian, and I do. In no time, we will be teaching them how to play Flight Club.

I am sorry to report that since he got home, Mr. Starek has

been having long, worried conversations with somebody at the courthouse about the fate of Halina's house. It is still locked up, under the control of the bank, and it sounds like they plan to sell it at auction—not just the house, but everything in it.

This alarming news is what finally prompts Emily to tell the old man that she and Michael have found a way to sneak in, and to ask him if he wants her to gather up a few of Halina's things for him to keep. She reminds him of the photos she took on her phone that first day we visited Halina's house. Are there any family mementos he wants?

Of course, the thing Mr. Starek wants most is the Pleyel piano, but that's too big to fit through the window, and the bank would definitely notice if that went missing. Mr. Starek says it would be wrong to take anything that had monetary value, because of the money Halina owed the bank. So he settles on a short list of things that would matter only to him: a ceramic dish where his father used to keep cuff links, a photograph of his mother with baby Halina and himself gathered on her lap, a small lamp with a colorful silk shade, and a framed drawing of the family home in Poland. He has seen all of these in Emily's photos, and now we have only to go back to Halina's house and get them.

So that is why, on a breezy day in September, Michael and Emily show up at Halina's house with an empty cardboard box and Mr. Starek's list of items. And of course I am there to watch. It seems impossible that the house could look shabbier and more neglected than the first time we saw it, but somehow it does. The giant locks and warning signs don't help. I think we are all feeling forlorn just contemplating it. This house is the last connection to Halina, who was the last connection to Mr. Starek's own childhood.

"Here," Emily says, showing Michael the list. "Let's do it quickly in case somebody from the bank surprises us. The photo and the drawing are in that first bedroom upstairs, where we found the painting of the piano. Can you get those? I'll get the lamp and the dish from downstairs."

"Sure," Michael says.

They push open the study window and boost themselves through. I wait in the rhododendron. Mostly, I look at the Pleyel, with its beautiful gleaming wood, its lustrous pattern of dapples and swirls. I wonder if this is the last time I'll see it. Who knows where it came from, or where it will end up after the bank sells it to some stranger?

"I've got the pictures," Michael calls, and I hear his feet thumping down the stairs.

"And I have the lamp and the dish," Emily says. She comes into the study, glancing around. "I hope there isn't anything special he's forgotten about. There's so much here."

"Yeah." Michael joins her. "But Mr. Starek's house wouldn't have room for all this stuff anyway." I can tell he's trying to make himself feel better.

Emily nods. "Even Halina's house didn't have room for it."

They lean over the windowsill and lower the pictures, the lamp, and the dish gently into the cardboard box.

Michael sits down on the piano bench and runs one hand over the keys. "Do you think I can still come over to play it? Until the auction?"

Emily considers this. "I don't see why not. I mean, you're not hurting anything, and if they catch us, what are they going to do? Just kick us out."

Michael is silent, staring at the Pleyel.

"I wish..."

Emily sighs. "Me too." She slides one leg over the windowsill and ducks her head. "We should go. Are you ready?"

"Yeah, I guess." Michael starts to follow her, then stops. "Wait—what about the painting?"

The painting of the Pleyel! Oh, take the painting. Mr. Starek hasn't even seen it. Surely if he had, he would have wanted that, too.

Michael crouches next to it. "If we can't take the piano, can we at least take the painting of the piano?"

Emily grimaces. "It's too big to fit through the window, isn't it?"

"Not if we turn it sideways," Michael says.

"Really?" Emily squints at the frame, and I see her point. It will be tight. But I want them to try.

Emily climbs through the open window and stands on the ground outside. "Can you bring it over here?"

Michael nods. He carefully drags the painting across the floor to the window. Emily reaches through and helps him lift it and tilt it on a diagonal.

I hold my breath. Will it squeeze through?

There is less than a quarter inch to spare at either end. But slowly, carefully, with Michael pushing and Emily pulling, they are able to slide the painting through the window.

"Yes!" Michael says. "Now we can show it to Mr. Starek."

"Shhhh," Emily cautions. "Help me put it in the trunk, quick. I don't want anyone to see us taking stuff out of the house."

Holding the painting awkwardly between them, they carry it to Emily's car and lay it flat in the trunk. Then Emily shoves the box of keepsakes onto the rear seat, and Michael runs back to close the study window. Time to go.

I get to Mr. Starek's house before they do, naturally, so I land in the yew bush by the front porch to watch what unfolds. I'm worried they'll take everything inside and I won't get to see the old man's reaction. But in fact, the painting is so large that Michael and Emily unload it first, carrying it to the front porch and leaning it against the side of the house. They get the box of other stuff from the car, and it's only then that they ring the bell.

It takes Mr. Starek a few minutes to answer. He moves more slowly since his illness.

He smiles when he sees the collection of things from Halina's. "Ah, thank you. I am glad to have these," he says, bending over the box. "I almost feel like I'm getting Halina back again through her things. It's as if something that ended between us has been allowed to continue."

Then he sees the painting.

He grips the doorframe, unsteady.

"It's from Halina's," Michael explains. "We found it upstairs. It's a painting of the Pleyel, our actual Pleyel. We can tell from—oh, so many things—but especially the patterns in the wood. And we thought—"

Mr. Starek hasn't taken his eyes off the painting. "I know what it is."

"What do you mean?" Emily asks.

"But it can't be," he says softly.

He steps out onto the sunny porch, and we are all watching him in confusion. It *is* strange that there's a painting of Halina's Pleyel piano—it's wonderful, really—but none of us were as shocked to see it as Mr. Starek appears to be.

The painting, which is very dark, looks much brighter out here in the daylight. It's possible to see all the shadings of brown in the piano's wooden surface, the intricate curls of color and light. I see the rough black patch framing the front of the piano, where the keys would be, and I notice again the brass florets studding the side, and the little bouquet of flowers, a cluster of color—dark reds and pinks and gold and white—on the top of the piano.

"What is it?" Michael asks. "Why are you so surprised?"

Mr. Starek is shaking his head, bending closer to the painting. "There! Do you see? In the corner?"

With a thin, trembling finger, he points to the far corner of the canvas.

Michael squats on the porch and squints at the textured, gleaming paint. "Yes," he says. "I think it's letters, but they're in cursive. It's hard for me to read cursive. Maybe *E...U...G*? And then a period. What does that mean?"

Yeah, what does that mean? *Eug*? What kind of word is that?

"It's true," Mr. Starek says, with a sharp intake of breath. "It's real."

"What?" Emily asks again. "Tell us! What?"

"*EUG* is short for *Eugene*. Eugene Dela—"

"Delacroix!" Emily gasps. "The painter? The friend of Chopin and George Sand?" She crouches down next to Michael. "Oh!"

They stare at each other.

"It says *Delacroix* right here," Emily whispers. "I can't believe we didn't see it."

Chopin's old friend, that famous painter! I remember—the one who stayed at George Sand's house in Nohant and talked about the beautiful garden and the birds singing. *He* painted this?

"It's the last fragment of the painting," the old man says, his voice hushed. "The third piece."

"You mean..." Michael stares at him.

"The portraits of Chopin and George Sand that we looked at on Emily's computer...they came from *this* canvas." Mr. Starek is shaking his head in amazement. "Remember how I told you it was cut into sections and sold? Well, the full picture was of Chopin playing his piano for George Sand. The missing piece was the piano."

"That's why you don't see the keyboard," Emily cries. "Because that black patch in front of the piano is Chopin! It's the rest of his portrait!"

Mr. Starek laughs in astonishment, and I realize I have never heard the old man laugh in all the while I've known him. "Nobody knew what happened to the remainder of the painting. But here it is! Delacroix painted this almost two hundred years ago, and Halina...my sister, Halina...she had it in her house all this time."

Michael jumps to his feet, his eyes wide. "But if the piano in the painting is the same as..."

We are all realizing it at the same time. The Pleyel!

Mr. Starek freezes. "You're sure it's a painting of *our* Pleyel? The exact same piano that is at Halina's house?"

"Yes!" Emily answers. "We compared them side by side. The designs in the wood are the same. If this is the same piano—"

Yes! Yes! I fly in circles over their heads, unable to stop myself.

Michael shouts triumphantly, "Halina's Pleyel must have belonged to Chopin!"

We know it now.

We know the truth.

The strange magic of the Pleyel was real. The way Michael played, the way he could feel the piano *showing* him how to play—well, those very keys had been stroked and tapped and banged by Frédéric Chopin.

But...oh! The Pleyel is locked inside Halina's house.

The bank is going to sell it.

Emily grabs Mr. Starek's arm. "If it's Chopin's piano—if this is a painting by Delacroix—we can't let the bank have them!"

"No, no, no, we can't," Mr. Starek says. "We can't even keep them for ourselves. They belong to history."

He looks at Emily and Michael, and I can see color flooding into his face, his eyes bright and clear.

"This changes everything," he says, his voice steady. "I need to make some phone calls."

36

Tree Full of Songs

And it does change everything. Apparently in the human world, old pianos played by famous composers and old paintings painted by famous artists are worth a great deal of money.

Money that can be used to pay off mortgages and bank loans and to reclaim a house.

Halina's house.

Halina's things.

Oh, it is so exciting! The thing we feared most is not going to happen, and the thing we wanted most just might!

After Mr. Starek makes his calls, over a series of days, there is a flurry of activity. Strangers come to his house, including people in vans with large cameras, and it appears that Mr.

Starek and Michael and Emily will be on *television*.

I would like to be on television, you know. It is all part of my dream to become a star. I think I would look quite fetching, don't you? Even if they say the TV camera adds ten pounds, which would be a lot on a little bird like me.

Mother is not at all happy about these comings and goings. She forbids us from approaching the house while there are so many strangers milling about. So I have to content myself with practicing my singing in the holly tree.

But this is tricky. I have never sung Chopin for my family. *Why not?* you're wondering. Well, at first, because it was a brand-new secret between Michael and me, something nobody else knew about. And then, because the more time I spent with the boy, the more I worried about saying or doing anything that would lead Mother to forbid it. And finally, because my duets with Michael had been going on for so long and had come to mean so much to me that it seemed impossible to admit to my mother and brothers that there was this big, important part of my life that I'd kept hidden from them. Secrets can start small, but they grow. What begins as a tiny decision to keep something quiet can send ripples through everything, like a stone landing in a pond.

But I don't want it to be a secret anymore. It makes me so happy, and they are my family, after all. How can I not share it with them?

I want to sing Chopin, and I want to sing it for my mother and brothers—and sisters!

So one day, I say to Mother, "Do you want to hear the music I learned while I was listening to Michael get ready for the competition?"

Mother is busy tidying the nest, which won't be needed soon. Lina, Serena, and George are starting to fly. She glances up, surprised. "What do you mean?"

I take a deep breath, unsure of her reaction. "I learned how to sing Chopin! With Michael."

"Piano music?" Mother stops replacing broken twigs and stares at me.

"Yes, Chopin," I say. "I want to sing it for you. All of you."

Sebastian has overheard and comes swooping down, with Oliver right behind him. "What are you talking about?" he demands. "What are you going to sing?"

"A concert," I tell them. "A classical music concert."

"Why would you sing that when you can sing our songs?" Sebastian demands. "Nothing is better than birdsong."

"This is different," I say. "Just listen."

"Wait," Mother says. "Let me get the girls." She lifts off from the nest and flies in small circles, calling my sisters, who are practicing their short flights from branch to branch of the holly tree.

Finally, everyone is gathered before me—Mother and the babies in the nest, Sebastian and Ollie perched next to it.

"Ready?" I say. "I'm going to sing you the three pieces Michael played at the Chopin Festival."

Now I have everyone's attention.

And then, for the second time, I give a concert for an audience that isn't Michael.

I confess, I am nervous at first. Will they even like the sound of it?

But as my voice finds the notes, first the prelude, then the étude, then the last ballade, the holly tree shimmers with music—the most divine, impossible music—and it becomes, truly, a tree full of songs.

Even the babies are riveted.

When I finish, they are all staring at me.

"Oh, Mirabelle!" Mother exclaims. "That was...well, I'm not sure I even have words for it. Those melodies were so complex—I can't believe you could master them. What a gift you have, darling."

A gift! Did you hear that? I always knew it. I'm an artist—an *artiste*—after all.

I tell them what each piece is called, and the babies clamor for more. "'Tree full of songs'! 'Tree full of songs'!" they cry.

My singing shudders the holly leaves and reverberates out into the whole backyard.

I'm warm from all that exertion, so when Ollie suggests we cool off in the birdbath, it sounds like a good idea. We fly across the yard to its stone edge, and I survey the reaches of this known, familiar world: the scrim of trees, the garden shed, the patio, the fence. It's the same as it was at the start of the summer, before Michael and Chopin. But it all looks different to me now.

Why is that? Maybe because *I'm* different. Maybe when you take something fully into your heart—an idea, a person, a passion—it changes you. It changes how you see the world.

My brothers and I dip and splash in the cool water, fluffing our feathers, sending arcs of sparkling droplets onto the lawn.

"You know what I think?" Sebastian says. "That music sounded good and all, but it took a lot of work."

"Well, yes," I admit. "It took practice."

"All the time you spent learning those songs," he continues, "you could've been doing fun stuff with Ollie and me. Think about what you missed."

Oliver nods. "He's right. Stop hanging around the old man's house so much, and do more things with *us*."

I do miss playing with my brothers. It will be good to have more time for this birdbath, and Flight Club, and exploring the neighborhood.

But as happy as I am to be spending time with my family, and to finally share Chopin with them, I miss Michael.

I realize that what I really want—what I really need—is to make music with Michael.

And I don't know when I will sing with him again. Or *if* I will.

37

Chopin Forever

But enough about me. I know you must be wondering what happened to the piano. It is the best news! As soon as the world found out that the Pleyel was Chopin's very own piano, everything changed. A lawyer in town offered to help Mr. Starek with the bank. The sale of Halina's house and her things was put on hold because it turned out her things were worth more—much, much more—than the money she owed the bank. Isn't that amazing? Her house really was a house full of treasures... only nobody knew it while she was alive. Would Halina have cared? I doubt it. I think she was happy just having her things for herself.

Mr. Starek explains that we can't keep the piano. It belongs to history. But fortunately, a very rich lady buys it and donates it to the Franklin Collection of Historical Instruments, the same place Emily told us about, a museum in the countryside near Boston. They are so excited to have a piano that once belonged to the great Frédéric Chopin. I mean, who wouldn't be? Everyone knows from the serial number and the date that this is the very piano Chopin used to compose the ballade in F minor—the last ballade, one of the most magnificent pieces of music ever written—over the course of one summer at George Sand's estate in Nohant. It is no wonder that Michael could feel the Pleyel teaching him how to play it.

Here's something even better: the director of the Franklin Collection has told Mr. Starek, Emily, and Michael that they may come play the Pleyel anytime they wish. Can you believe it? That's how I know Michael will always be able to play Chopin's piano.

Which makes me so happy. Although I must admit I am thinking: Can I come, too?

And I know you're wondering about the painting. The piece of the Delacroix canvas that shows the piano has been bought by the Louvre, a big, fancy art museum in Paris. It has one of the other fragments—not the part of the painting that shows George Sand, which is in a museum in Denmark, but the portrait of Chopin. Mr. Starek says the Louvre will hang these two pieces of the painting next to each other.

So Chopin will be reunited with his piano! His long-lost piano, which *we* found. I like thinking about that.

Do you know what else I like thinking about? Maybe the flowers in the painting, in the little vase on top of the piano, were flowers from the garden at George Sand's house in Nohant. Maybe they were picked by George Sand herself, and put there for Chopin to enjoy while he played. So even if the third piece of the painting, the one that portrays George Sand, can't hang alongside the others, at least she is there in a way, through her flowers.

It's on a warm day at the end of September that Michael shows up at Mr. Starek's house, with Emily. The television crews have left; the piano and the painting are gone. It's just us again, which feels right and good.

I am perched in the silk tree by the window of the music room, and Michael sees me as soon as he walks in. He comes straight to the window and smiles at me. I tilt my head and hop down the branch, closer to him.

What now? What next?

So much has happened, but the festival is behind us.

"I'm so glad you've come," Mr. Starek says to Michael and Emily, resting one hand on the Érard. "I wasn't sure I'd see you again now that our work is finished."

"Oh!" Emily exclaims. "Of course you'd see us again."

Michael looks alarmed. "I was always going to come back. And anyway, now I have to get ready for the competition in Poland next spring."

Mr. Starek smiles. "That's true. We will have to pick out new Chopin pieces for you to play."

"Yes." Michael nods vigorously.

New pieces! He may need some help with those.

Emily looks at me now, a slow smile lighting her face. I do a pretty little dance for her, hopping from branch to branch through the leaves of the silk tree. The blossoms have fallen, so it's easier for her to see me.

Michael stands over the piano bench. "Can I—" He hesitates.

"What is it?" Mr. Starek asks.

"I mean, I know I'm not here for a lesson, but if it's okay, could I warm up? The way I used to?"

Mr. Starek pats his shoulder. "Alone, you mean? Of course you may. Emily and I will enjoy listening from the kitchen."

Emily glances over her shoulder at me as they leave the room, and I think how these three are like my family now. My human family.

When the door closes, Michael and I are finally alone.

He comes over to the window, looking at me so intently I feel the walls and glass disappear.

"Guess what, Mirabelle," he says. I hop to the end of the branch and gaze into his dark eyes so he knows I'm listening.

"My dad is coming home!" he whispers. "Next weekend. For a long time."

Oh, isn't that wonderful? I know how happy it makes Michael, without him saying another word.

"He misses me," Michael continues. "He wants to hear me play all the pieces I played at the festival."

Good! It will be like the private concert I gave *my* family. Now Mr. Jin will have a chance to hear how much Chopin means to Michael.

Michael leans his face close to mine. "I'm so glad I met you," he says.

Well, I am, too! What would I be without Michael, or Michael without me? Look what we've become together.

I fly in a small, happy circle in front of his face.

"Ready?" Michael asks, turning back to the piano bench.

He sits, his hands hovering over the keys. What will he play?

I recognize the fast, cheery notes of the Minute Waltz as soon as the boy begins, and my whole heart shivers with joy.

The music courses through me.

I open my beak and *SING*.

Author's Note

Anyone who likes mysteries is a bit of a detective, so now that you've finished the book, I suspect you're wondering which parts of the story were real, and which parts I made up. Maybe as you were reading, you started doing a little research yourself, about birds and pianos, Chopin and George Sand. I hope so!

While all of the present-day characters in the story are the products of my imagination, the historical ones are real, and the details about their lives are true...even small details, like the one about George Sand's grandfather selling goldfinches on the streets of France. (You can imagine how happy I was when I came across that little gem in my research!)

Frédéric Chopin, "the poet of the piano," was a musical genius whose compositions for the piano—even in the nearly two centuries since his death—have no equals. He devoted himself to that particular instrument; all of his compositions were written for it. Both in his style of playing and in his method of teaching piano, Chopin emphasized the twin aims of discipline and innovation. As precise and exact as he was in composing, his goal was a sense of free, spontaneous expression, whether he was conveying playful joy or deep sorrow. He liked to play the piano in the dark, knowing the keys by touch alone. Though he died at the young age of thirty-nine, and gave only thirty public concerts in his life, Chopin's impact on the world of classical music was immense.

Chopin's relationship with George Sand profoundly shaped his life, and his time with her spanned the period of his greatest musical achievements. She was his girlfriend, his muse, his friend, and eventually his nurse and caregiver, but in all these roles, she thoroughly supported him as an artist. In her own way, Sand was as much of an innovator as Chopin. She separated from her husband at a time when divorce in France was illegal, and took a man's name, attire, and habits (such as cigar smoking) as she worked to establish herself as a writer. She achieved fame with more than sixty novels, two dozen plays, and many short stories, nonfiction pieces, and political essays.

Eugene Delacroix was a great friend of Chopin's and George Sand's, and he really did paint a large canvas depicting Chopin at the piano with Sand sitting behind him, listening reverently. Two sections of it, the separate portraits of Chopin and Sand, are in European museums, as described in the book. It is believed that the part of the canvas showing the piano was never completed, so that is where I took some artistic license—especially since the Delacroix painting actually showed an upright piano, and the earlier portions were completed in 1838. For the purposes of my story, I'm imagining that Delacroix finished the painting years later, adding the 1842 Pleyel.

What about the Pleyel in my story? As described, the Pleyel company ledgers are available online to researchers, and it's possible to look up pianos by their serial numbers. Alain Kohler has written extensively about the fates of Chopin's various pianos, several of which have been discovered in private homes and are now exhibited in museums around the world, as described in my story. Kohler believes that serial number 9164, a grand piano in dappled mahogany, was the instrument Chopin played in the summer of 1842, when he composed the last ballade at George Sand's estate in Nohant. That piano has yet to be found.

As far as Michael's piano festival, there are several piano competitions held around the world that focus exclusively on Chopin, and there really is a museum of antique pianos, the inspiration for my Franklin Collection. It's called the Frederick Collection of Historical Pianos, located in Ashburnham, Massachusetts. It houses Pleyels, Érards, and other amazing instruments dating from the 1790s to the 1920s. One of the owners, Patricia Frederick, was kind enough to give me a tour and to play for me on a gorgeous Pleyel from the 1840s so I could hear the sound that Chopin loved, and that wooed him away from every other type of piano. By prior arrangement, the Fredericks allow pianists to play the historical pianos in their collection so that they can experience musical pieces from long ago the way their composers intended.

Finally, you are probably wondering about the birds, Mirabelle and her family of goldfinches. The details about bird diets, habits, predators, and life cycles are all true. However, with songbirds, it is the males who sing most impressively, so Mirabelle's talent in this story would be even more extraordinary. Also, goldfinch fathers are usually very present and helpful in the rearing of their young; the absence of Mirabelle's father would be unusual.

As to their music: Could a goldfinch actually sing Chopin? Or any classical music, for that matter? Well, many birds are expert mimics, quite capable of copying musical phrases. It is said that Mozart had a starling he adopted as a pet because he heard it singing the opening bars of his Piano Concerto no. 17; presumably the bird had learned the tune from hearing Mozart play it. Quite recently, scientists have discovered that songbirds have a complex musical repertoire, an ability to balance repetition and novelty, to innovate and create, all while maintaining tone and tempo—a skill previously thought to be limited to humans. It does not seem a stretch to view birds as little musicians, or as musical artistes, as Mirabelle likes to call herself. Certainly, their songs have an equal capacity to fill us with wonder and delight.

Acknowledgments

All my novels are labors of love, but this one holds a special place in my heart. It drew me back to the world of my novel *Masterpiece*, where humans and animals form deep friendships—but this time, with a bird as my guide. Once I started writing from a goldfinch's point of view, I seemed to encounter those little yellow birds everywhere. I walk my dog in a nature preserve near my house and I would often see three or four goldfinches soaring over the wildflower meadows. Especially when I was at a tricky part of the story, I imagined that they were Mirabelle and her family, urging me to keep going.

This book took shape over several years, and during that time, a number of people made essential contributions. I am deeply grateful to the following:

- My beloved editor, Christy Ottaviano, who is as gifted at editing as Mirabelle is at singing, and who brought not just a sharp eye but a warm and embracing heart to this project.

- My agent, Edward Necarsulmer IV, who facilitated my transition with Christy to Little, Brown, where the entire team, from Editorial to Design to Marketing and Sales, has worked so hard to bring this book's best self to the world.

- Patricia Frederick of the Frederick Collection of Historical Pianos in Ashburnham, Massachusetts, who generously shared her wealth of knowledge about the pianos of Chopin's era—down to such details as serial number locations—and played both an Érard and a Pleyel for me so I could hear the differences in tone firsthand.

- My friend Jane Kamensky, whose musical expertise was invaluable to me. I took piano lessons growing up but had nowhere near Michael's musical aptitude—whereas Jane, happily, does. Her close reading of the music-related passages helped me navigate that aspect of the story.

- My wonderful community of writer friends, for the many conversations about story structure and writing process that have vastly improved my books: Sunita Apte, Donna Freitas, Ramin Ganeshram, Tommy Greenwald, Emily Jenkins, Victoria Kann, Alan Katz, Bennett Madison, Natalie Standiford, Lauren Tarshis, Chris Tebbetts, Hans Wilhelm, Ellen Wittlinger, and Lisa Yee.

- My dear friends and Vermont writing retreat pals, Jane Kamensky and Jill Lepore, who have companioned so much of my writing life, not to mention my real life.

- Sheila Clancy, Meg Cerbone, and my cousin Laura Broach for sharing their pretty homes on Cape Cod and Martha's Vineyard, where much of this book was written and revised.

- My amazing manuscript readers, who give so much time and thought to my rough drafts, and whose contributions shine on every page: Mary Broach, Jane Burns, Claire Carlson, Laura Forte, Jane Kamensky, Carol Sheriff, Ben Daileader Sheriff, Zoe Wheeler, and Grace Wheeler.

- And finally, a huge thank-you to my family, who makes everything worth it: Zoe, Harry, Grace, and of course Truman.

ELISE BROACH

is the *New York Times* bestselling author of nearly thirty books for children and young adults, including *Masterpiece*, *Shakespeare's Secret*, *The Wolf Keepers*, the Superstition Mountain trilogy, and the picture books *When Dinosaurs Came with Everything* and *My Pet Wants a Pet*. She is a two-time recipient of the E. B. White Read Aloud Award, and her books have received numerous honors, including an IRA Teachers' Choice Award and several ALA and NCTE Notable Book Awards. Elise lives in Connecticut near a meadow full of goldfinches. She invites you to visit her online at elisebroach.com.